KU-530-843

OVERKILL AT SADDLEROCK

Sheriff Seth Rossiter knew that if he didn't see Duke Finley safely in prison, he was in for bad trouble. For Finley had once been a close friend, and evil gossip had it that Rossiter might allow Duke to escape, and share in the still unrecovered fortune from the bank robbery Finley had pulled.

So when Finley broke free with the aid of a treacherous woman and a conniving gambler, Rossiter had to pursue three criminals on a wild chase that led to Saddlerock—to betrayal, bloodshed, and death . . .

OVERKILL AT SADDLEROCK

Ray Hogan

20173115

MORAY COUNCIL
LIBRARIES &
INFORMATION SERVICES

GUNSMOKE

First published in the UK by Chivers Press

This hardback edition 2007
by BBC Audiobooks Ltd
by arrangement with
Golden West Literary Agency

Copyright © 1979 by Ray Hogan.
All rights reserved.

ISBN 978 1 405 68129 2

British Library Cataloguing in Publication Data available.

20174185

MORAY COUNCIL
LIBRARIES &
INFORMATION SERVICES

WF

Printed and bound in Great Britain by
Antony Rowe Ltd., Chippenham, Wiltshire

to my friend

WILLIAM HOLMES

OVERKILL
AT
SADDLEROCK

★ 1 ★

Rigid, dark features set, Seth Rossiter faced Deputy U.S. Marshal J.W. Hill from across the desk. As sheriff of the county, with his office in the town of Cherryville—so named because of the abundance of chokecherry trees in the area—Rossiter had waged a constant battle with Hill over the federal lawman's attempts to infringe on his authority.

"I'll get Duke Finley to the pen!" he snapped, voice fairly crackling. "Don't fret about it!"

Hill, a man somewhere in his fifties, thinning gray hair neatly combed and parted, stood with his hat in hand and stared off into the dusty street. It was unusually warm for late spring, and the vest of his velvet-lapeled brown suit was unbuttoned halfway down. That was his only concession to the heat, however, for his checked shirt was closed at the neck with a starched collar and string tie.

"Whatever you say, Sheriff," he said stiffly, and raising his hat, placed it squarely on his head. "Only aiming to help. The governor's got a real special interest in Finley, since that money him and Brodie stole ain't never been found."

From a position near the door that opened into the

cell block, Burt Antrum, Rossiter's deputy, said: "I've heard that he'll pardon Duke if he'll tell where they stashed that thirty thousand dollars. That true?"

Hill's shoulders stirred. "Can't say. Maybe. All I know is that it's mighty important Finley gets to the pen. Now, I'll only be gone a week, Sheriff. I'm suggesting that you hold off taking him to Pottstown till I get back and can go with you. A few more days won't make one whit difference to the warden—"

"Makes a difference to me!" Rossiter declared flatly. "I'll be heading out today with him."

As if striving to break the tension mounting steadily within the small, stuffy room and keep matters between the two lawmen on an even keel, Antrum crossed leisurely to a window and settled himself on the sill.

"The sheriff figures to take the old road, the one east of the mountains," he said conversationally. "Ain't hardly no traveling done on it nowadays and he thinks there'll be less chance of trouble."

Hill's forehead creased into a frown. "Trouble? You expecting trouble, Sheriff?"

Rossiter flung a rebuking glance at the deputy and shook his head. A tall, raw-boned man nearing thirty, he had deep-set eyes, a hard mouth, and an angular face. He was wearing a flat-crowned black hat, and while he, too, affected a collar and tie, he was coatless, wearing instead a vest upon which he had pinned his star. The legs of his gray cord pants were tucked inside his boots, in preparation for riding.

"No more trouble than a man can look for when he's moving a prisoner," he said coolly. "There's always the possibility that a friend—or maybe an enemy—will take it in mind to try something."

"You for sure there ain't nothing certain?"

"No, nothing certain!" Rossiter declared, adding impatiently, "hell, I know my job! And I never take chances with a prisoner!"

"I ain't saying you do," Hill replied tartly. "And

2

taking a back road's smart as long as it don't get nosed around." The lawman paused, and for a brief time listened to the distant pounding of a hammer. Then, "You want me to come straight to the point, Sheriff?"

Rossiter shifted, leaned back against the wall, and folded his arms across his chest. He had planned to leave early for Pottstown, where the penitentiary was located—had his horse saddled and ready to go, as was Finley's—but Hill delayed him.

"Up to you," he said indifferently.

"Well, it's that you and Finley used to be real close friends," the marshal said. "You two done a lot of cowboying together before you took up being a lawman and he went bad. A lot of folks know that."

Seth Rossiter had stiffened and his eyes had narrowed. "So?" he pressed.

"I ain't meaning no offense—and I'm only telling you what's on some folks' minds—"

Two riders rushed by, the hoofs of their horses raising an echo that drummed along the street and started dust to drifting lazily along its length.

"Come on, Hill—out with it!"

"Well, they're saying that you two being such good friends once, that maybe you might take it in your head to feel sorry for Duke and just let him get loose—escape."

Seth Rossiter made no immediate comment. Then, in a controlled voice that did not reveal the anger surging through him, he said, "Who're these people you're calling 'they'?"

"That's fool talk!" Burt Antrum stated loyally before the marshal could reply. "The sheriff ain't about to do nothing like that! I been a deputy for—"

"That's the way I see it, too," Hill cut in, ignoring Rossiter's question. "You're too good a lawman to ever pull a stunt like that, but I figured you ought to know what you can expect if something goes wrong."

"Like what?" Rossiter asked.

"What I just told you—you lose Duke Finley, even if it ain't your fault, folks'll be wondering whether you sort of made it easy for him. Big reason why I offered to go along with you. Be no question then if something happened and he got away."

"He won't," Rossiter said, unrelenting. "You can tell that to those people you keep mentioning. And you can say that I'll get Duke to the pen alive if I can, dead if I have to."

"Sure, I'm—"

"And something else, Marshal, I sure as hell don't appreciate talk like that. I've never dirtied my badge in my life and I sure as hell don't aim to start this late in the game with some two-bit outlaw like Duke Finley!"

"I believe you, but folks maybe are thinking about that money he's got cached somewheres—they're thinking it, not me—and that he just might buy you off with a big chunk of it."

Rossiter's jaw hardened. His dark eyes narrowed into glowing slits in the sun-browned planes of his face. "Get the hell out of my office, Hill!" he shouted. "I've heard enough of your supposing."

The federal marshal only smiled. "It's real insulting, I know, and I reckon it's tromping on your pride a-plenty. But I figured you ought to know how folks feel. There ain't nothing personal in it far as I'm concerned, Sheriff. You got to remember that."

"I'll remember it," Rossiter said, his voice still taut. He abruptly swung toward Antrum. "Both horses ready?"

The deputy nodded. "Waiting out back, all fixed up just like you wanted. Didn't put no grub—"

Rossiter, removing his collar and tie and replacing them with a red bandanna, said: "Won't be needing any. Can eat at the towns along the way."

"That back road—it's going to take you ten, maybe eleven days' riding," Hill went on, refusing to be ignored. "That's one hell of a long time to be in the

4

saddle with a prisoner that everybody knows has got a big passel of money hid out."

Rossiter grinned humorlessly. "But then everybody won't know I'm taking him up the back road—unless you spread it around."

It was J. W. Hill's turn to become angry. He brushed at his mustache, and taking up his rifle, hung it in the crook of an arm.

"All right, Sheriff—have it your way!" he snapped, moving toward the door. "I'm just hoping nothing bad happens, because if you lose your prisoner, you've lost your standing, and your time as a lawman'll be over. You'll for sure never be able to convince folks that you didn't let Finley go."

Seth's mouth pulled into a wry smile. "A man's word and his reputation for honesty don't count for anything—that what you're saying?"

"In your case it won't, because you and Finley was once bunkies—and maybe you owed him a favor. But I'm done talking about it—you do what you want. I've got my own job to take care of—and if you're too damn bullheaded to hold off till I can give you a hand, then so be it."

"So be it, Marshal," Rossiter said quietly, anger still pulsing within him, and nodded to Antrum. "Bring him out, Burt. I'm running late and I want to get started."

As the deputy turned to fetch the prisoner, Hill paused in the doorway and looked back.

"Luck," he called over his shoulder.

"Obliged—and same to you," Rossiter replied, but the federal lawman was already out on the landing and turning away.

★ 2 ★

"We a-going bye-bye, papa?" Duke Finley asked in a derisive tone as, followed by Deputy Antrum, he came through the doorway that led from the cell block into the sheriff's office.

He was grinning broadly, and Antrum, shaking his head in wonderment, said, "Don't you never take nothing serious, Duke? You're always funning. . . . Put your hands behind you."

The outlaw halted in the center of the room, and doing as the deputy directed, continued to grin while the lawman joined his wrists with chain and cuffs.

"Hell no—not me!" he said finally. "Why should I? A man never gets out of this life alive, so it's plain everyday horse sense to have a good time while you're still around. Ain't that so, Seth?"

Rossiter made no reply, simply waited until the manacles had been locked in place. Then, eyeing the outlaw critically, he said, "He got any other clothes back there?"

Finley, dark-haired, blue-eyed, and sporting a full mustache, was a good-looking man—even handsome by some standards. He possessed an easy-going, engaging personality, which made it easy for him to form friendships, particularly where women were concerned, and which, conversely, probably accounted for most of the serious trouble he'd gotten himself into during his life.

Dressed now in a red woolen shirt, yellow neckerchief, lightweight brown duck pants tucked into boots decorated with yellow stitching, and a Texas peaked hat, he appeared to be heading for a good time somewhere rather than for the Territorial Penitentiary, where he was to spend the next twenty years of his life.

"Had a brush jacket. I tied it on his saddle," Antrum replied. "Got yours wrapped up in your slicker behind the cantle, too. You didn't say nothing about coffee so I put some in your saddlebags just the same—along with a pot and a couple of cups. Ain't no grub—"

"Hell, you planning on starving me?" Duke demanded in mock indignation.

"We'll eat when and where we get the chance," Rossiter said. "I don't figure to spend much time camping. We'll be on the move most of the time."

"You mean we ain't making all them saloons and bedding all them pretty women that we'll be coming to between here and Pottstown—like we used to?" Finley said in exaggerated surprise.

"Not about to," the lawman said, motioning at the door leading to the rear of the jail.

"Seth, you sure have changed," Duke declared mournfully. "Was the day when you'd—"

"Move," Rossiter cut in sharply, and laying a hand on the outlaw's shoulder, pushed him roughly. "I want to be halfway to Cougar Ridge by dark."

Burt Antrum was right; Duke never took anything seriously—but then he had always been that way, and being so had made him a good partner on the trail. As some one had said once, Duke Finley was the kind that'd greet the devil with a joke when the moment of their meeting came.

They moved through the doorway out into the yard

behind the building, where two horses, loaded for the journey, were waiting patiently in the shade of a cottonwood tree. Duke halted beside the gray that had been provided for his use.

"I reckon one of you gents'll have to boost me up onto the saddle—me being sort of hobbled," he said.

Antrum stepped up to the outlaw, helped him onto the gray. The deputy turned questioningly to Rossiter, who was settling himself on his mount.

"You aiming to leave him ride that a-way—his hands behind him? He can't hold the lines—"

"Won't need to," the sheriff said, tossing a short length of rope to the young lawman. "Tie that to the gray's bit ring. I'll be leading him."

Duke swore, then grinned. "I sure can't recollect ever being so comfortable! If'n it's all right with you, Mister Sheriff, why I'll just ride this way clean to the pen."

"Just what you'll do," Rossiter said unfeelingly, and put his flat glance on Antrum. "There anything on your mind?"

The deputy shook his head. "Nope. I'll just set tight and keep an eye on things around here till you get back."

"Right," Seth said. "Anything comes up in the county, just let it hang. I'll look into it when I get back. I don't want you leaving town."

"I savvy. Howsomever, if something real important turns up, you want me calling in J. W. Hill if he's around?"

Rossiter gave that thought, shrugged. "Only if it's something that can't wait. . . . So long."

"So long, Sheriff—good luck," Antrum replied as the lawman and his prisoner pulled away from the tree and moved off.

"He's a right nice fellow," Duke said, and then laughed. "But you always was real good at picking your friends—like me, for a sample."

Rossiter made no comment, and keeping to the rear of the buildings on the west side of the street, led the way to the edge of the town and onto the road that cut its way north.

"This sure reminds me of the old days, Seth," Duke said, twisting about and looking back.

The lawman shrugged. Among Finley's many accomplishments, he recalled, he was also a constant talker.

"How so?"

"Makes me remember us when we was punching cows and would be heading for home after raising hell all night in some stinking saloon. Man, we sure used to have us a time!"

"Expect we did," Rossiter agreed. "Too bad it ended."

"Yep, I reckon things might've turned out different if we'd kept on riding together—but you making up your mind to wear a star like you did, well, it sort of left me high and dry."

"Maybe, but that was no reason for you to start hanging out with Rube Brodie and his kind."

"Hell, there just wasn't nothing else to do!"

"You could've gone on cowpunching, same as we'd been doing."

They were now well clear of Cherryville and moving across a barren flat known as Pedrogoso Mesa toward a lengthy band of trees and brush through which the road cut its way. It was hot in the open and both men were showing the effect of the driving sun, and looking forward to the relief that would come when they reached and entered the grove with its giant cottonwoods and other growth.

"No, you pulling out sort of drove my liking for that kind of work right out of my head," Duke said. "Man punches cows, he's got to have a good sidekick to do it with."

9

"I don't remember you ever having trouble making friends," Rossiter commented dryly.

Duke laughed. "No, I reckon I sure didn't—not the kind that wears pants or the kind that wear a dress, either! Say, Seth, you recollect that time over in Fort Worth when we took in a barn dance and you got yourself in a whole peck of trouble?"

"Yeh, sure do—"

"Was over a little gal, one that some ranchhand was all set to marry up with. He didn't cotton much to your shining up to her, and him and a couple of his friends decided to let you know that. Time I could turn loose of my gal, they had you down and was pounding hell out of you."

"I'm not apt to forget it," Rossiter said, brushing at the sweat on his forehead. He had a hunch as to what was coming next, but he said no more.

"You know," Duke said, shifting to ease his shoulders, "I expect they'd a-beat you to death if I hadn't been around to jump in and pull them off you! Them Texans don't take kindly to strangers messing with their women."

"I was in a tight spot, for sure," the lawman agreed.

"Guess it could be said you sort of owe me a favor."

Rossiter shrugged, again swiped at the sweat on his face. "Never been much of a hand to keep books on such, since it works both ways, but—"

"What I'm getting at, Seth—it sure does work both ways! And figuring what good friends we always was, I'm asking a favor right now. How about taking off these danged handcuffs when we get in the trees and stop to make coffee. Then, when you're sort of busy and looking the other way, I'll light out."

It was just the way J. W. Hill had figured it could work out. A hard smile cracked Seth Rossiter's lips as he recalled the marshal's words. "Just turn you loose—let you escape, that it?" he said, looking directly at Finley.

"Be just that easy. Hell, we ain't but forty miles from the Mexican border! By this time tomorrow I'd be across it and long gone!"

"How'd I explain letting you escape to the governor?"

"Well, you could say there was an accident of some sort, or maybe—"

"Forget it, Duke," Rossiter cut in harshly, suddenly tired of the subject. "You know I won't do it."

"Not even for a man who was your best friend and done you plenty of good turns?"

"Not for anybody," the lawman replied.

They had reached the first of the trees and were entering the grove. The immediate coolness was apparent.

Finley heaved a deep sigh. "I sure ain't looking forward to them twenty years in the pen. That's a mighty long time for a fellow to be cooped up."

Rossiter nodded his agreement. "Best thing you can do is get with the warden once you're settled in at the pen, say you want to see the governor, that you're willing to tell him where you and Brodie stashed the money you stole if he'll shorten your sentence. He might even pardon you since it was Brodie that killed that bank teller during the robbery, as I understand it."

"Yeh, was Rube," Duke said, spirits undampened despite the lawman's refusal to go along with his escape plan. "And old Rube was mighty sorry he had to do it. Just about the last thing he said before he died, after we took off into the hills, was that he hated doing it but that he had to because the danged fool went for a gun."

Rossiter was only half listening. Far ahead, on the shoulder of the road, he could see a horse. The saddle was empty and there was no sign of a rider anywhere nearby.

"Seth, you be interested in a little deal?" Duke continued. "Ain't no use trying to fool you, because you already know about that money—thirty thousand dollars worth—and it's just waiting for me to come get it. Now, if you and me could work together, sort of be partners again, I'd sure be willing to do some sharing."

They had topped out a rise and the horse's rider had come into sight—a crumpled shape sprawled in the center of the dusty road.

"Shut up, Duke! I'm telling you again—forget it!" Rossiter snapped impatiently.

Suspicion was building within him as he studied the motionless figure. It could be someone in need of help, or it might be a trick, one conceived by friends of the outlaw and designed to take the outlaw from him—and he wanted no distractions while he made certain which.

"Just keep your lip buttoned till I see what this up ahead's all about," he added.

★ 3 ★

"Looks like somebody's got hurt—throwed from a horse," Duke said, focusing his attention on the unconscious rider.

Rossiter had pulled the horses down to a slow walk. He was taking no chances. If it was a trick, he was not about to be taken unaware. Eyes moving back and forth, he searched the brush on either side of the road for indications of others hiding in the deep brush. He could see nothing else but the solitary horse standing at the edge of the road.

It was a woman, Seth Rossiter saw moments later when he drew nearer. She lay on her side, legs doubled, arms thrown forward, her face turned down.

"She's sure needing help," Duke said. "If you want I'll climb down—"

"Stay in your saddle!" the lawman ordered as they drew abreast the prostrate figure and passed slowly by.

He was irritated by the prospect of being held back, of being confronted by a delay that could require his returning to the settlement with the injured woman.

"Ain't you going to help her?" Duke asked in a shocked voice. "Hell, Seth, this ain't like you—turning

13

your back on a hurt woman, leaving her laying in the road where—"

Rossiter swore angrily, again scanned the brush for signs of a trap. He saw nothing that was not in order, and cutting sharply about, rode up to one of the smaller nearby trees.

"Stay where you are," he said tautly, nodding to Finley as he dismounted. "I'll see if I can do anything for her."

Tying the outlaw's horse securely to the sapling, and leaving his own mount a few steps beyond, Rossiter hurried back to the road, his eyes continuing their restless search of the surrounding vicinity. It appeared to be an accident—the horse probably having shied and thrown the woman from his back—but Seth Rossiter was finding himself wary and unable to shake the feeling that there was something amiss, that all wasn't as it should be.

He reached the woman, glanced down. Her hat lay off to one side, and thick dark hair had spilled about her face and neck. She was a pretty one, he saw, and noted also that she was wearing a man's clothing.

Rossiter threw a quick look at the horse. The saddlebags were full and straining at the buckles, and behind the cantle he could see a blanket roll, a slicker, and what probably was a jacket. The lawman frowned. Evidently the woman was not from some ranch nearby since she was packed for traveling; but a woman on that deserted road alone?

She groaned, stirred. Rossiter, hand resting on the butt of his pistol as he considered the waiting horse, shifted his attention quickly to the woman. She was alive, and perhaps—unless she had sustained some broken bones—was uninjured. Given a little water to drink and a wet handkerchief for application to her forehead, maybe she could make it on to Cherryville, only ten or twelve miles, on her own. Bending low, the lawman took her by a shoulder and gently turned her onto her back.

"She dead?" Duke called.

Rossiter shook his head, reached for the bandanna in his back pocket. He'd soak in with water from his canteen, bathe her face. That should bring her around.

He started to rise, checked abruptly as the woman's arms suddenly went around his neck. The lawman, in the act of drawing himself upright, was caught off balance. Jerking hard, she caused him to fall forward across her—but alarm was already racing through him and he was reaching for his pistol even as her weight dragged him down.

Anger gripped him. It was a trick—but they didn't have him yet! He went flat on top of the woman, his body at right angles to hers. Rossiter heard breath explode from her throat as he crushed her—but he gave that no thought. His sole intention was to get clear of her, and pistol in hand, be ready for whatever came next.

And then the quick rap of heels reached him as he fought to get free of the woman's arms and struggle to his feet. A fraction of time later he felt a solid blow to the head, and coming with the pain it brought, total darkness.

★ 4 ★

"It's sure good to see you, Nella," Duke Finley yelled as he slid from his horse. His hands locked together behind him, he hurried to the center of the road.

The woman had pulled herself from under Seth Rossiter's body and risen to her feet. She glanced at the outlaw and smiled. Pretty, well built, with jet-black hair and matching eyes, she had altered the male clothing she was wearing to more feminine lines by narrowing the pant legs and taking in the shirt.

"It's been a while," she said as she dusted herself with her hat. "You've changed."

Duke grinned. "Laying around inside a calaboose for a couple of months don't do a man no good." He paused, glanced at the tall blond man standing silent near Seth Rossiter's unconscious figure. "Who's he?"

Nella Brodie half turned, and smiled at the man, who was still holding the pistol with which he had knocked the lawman senseless. "Name's Ferd Kissler," she said. "Good friend of mine. Helped me a-plenty since Rube died—helped me set this up so's we could take you away from that john law, in fact."

Kissler had the pale, expressionless eyes and the stilled manner of a gambler. He was well dressed—

16

dark shirt, red bandanna, leather vest, cord pants, and almost new black boots. A nugget of green jade hung from a rawhide string around his neck.

"Well, if you helped Nella you're sure aces with me," Duke said in a booming voice. "I'd be right pleased to shake your hand but I'm kind of tied up now."

Nella smiled again, jerked her head at Ferd. "Get the keys to the cuffs. Probably in the sheriff's shirt pocket."

Kissler holstered his weapon and bent over Rossiter. Rummaging through the lawman's pockets briefly, he produced two keys on a small round ring, and stepping up to Finley, who had turned about, removed the manacles.

Immediately, Duke wheeled to the woman, and throwing his arms about her, implanted a kiss on her lips. Laughing, he stepped back.

"Been wanting to do that ever since you hitched up with Rube, only I didn't have the sand."

Nella stared at him for several moments, and then smiled. "Well, I'll say this—it took you long enough!"

Duke, chafing his wrists to restore circulation, grinned broadly. "That mean you've maybe done some thinking about me—about you and me, I mean?"

"Many times," Nella said, and glanced about. "We best drag the sheriff off the road, hadn't we? Somebody might come along, see us."

"For sure," Duke said, and gave Kissler a side look. "I reckon he can ride on now, can't he? We're done with him."

Nella Brodie frowned, brushed at a lock of hair that had come loose from the rest, now tucked up inside her hat.

"Well, no. I had to promise him a share of the money for helping me. I couldn't do all this alone—"

"That's sure a new song!" Duke said. "Ain't never before heard of you needing help to do something!"

"I suppose so—but this was different. I didn't have any money to work with, and we needed horses and supplies, things like that."

"Still don't see why he needs to hang around. I was figuring strong on it being just me and you—together from here on out. You just don't know how much I been wanting you! Why, laying around in that jail—"

"I know," Nella cut in quickly. "And it'll turn out just like you hoped, but we'll have to let him string along with us till we get the money. Then we can pay him off—that's what I promised. Where is the money? Is it close by?"

Duke wagged his head. "Nope, it's a far piece from here," he said, mopping at the sweat on his brow.

"Does that mean several days?"

"More like a couple of weeks, maybe a little less," Duke said, and turned his attention to Nella's horse. "You fetch a gun and belt for me?"

"In my saddlebags," she replied, moving off. "Got some money for you, too—thirty dollars or so. I'll get it while you and Ferd drag the sheriff off the road and into the brush, where you can get rid of him."

Duke, reaching down for Rossiter's ankles preparatory to moving him, hesitated, looked up at the gambler.

"We ain't killing him—"

"The hell we ain't!" Kissler snapped. "Can't have no lawman dogging our tracks."

Nella, overhearing, had paused. Frowning darkly, she dropped back a few steps. "What's come over you, Duke? Since when did putting a bullet in a tin badge get on your don't-do list?"

"There just ain't no need—"

A half smile parted the woman's lips. "I savvy now. This sheriff's sort of special with you because you and him used to ride together. I remember now you telling Rube and me how the two of you did so much hell raising and had such good times before he got religion and turned lawman. He's the one, ain't he?"

Finley nodded. "But that ain't all. Seth was plenty good to me while I was in his jail—sort of favored me, in fact. I figure I owe him something for that."

"Well, I sure'n hell don't owe him nothing!" Ferd Kissler declared, and drawing his pistol, pointed it at Rossiter's head.

Duke threw himself forward, knocked the weapon aside, and sent Kissler stumbling backward off the road. "Damn you!" he shouted, thoroughly angry for one of the few times in his life. "You ain't doing nothing unless I say so! I want you to get that straight, Kissler; I'm the boss of this outfit—you ain't nothing but the hired help! From now on you keep your lip buttoned tight or, by God, I'll button it for you!"

Kissler had recovered his balance, and features bleak, was staring at Duke with cold, empty eyes. He stirred slightly, flicked Nella with a glance. Apparently reading something in her expression, he shrugged, slid his pistol back into its oiled holster, and folded his arms across his chest.

Finley also relaxed, produced a smile. "It ain't only that Seth's a friend of mine," he said, "it's something else that'd make it a fool stunt. There's a U.S. Marshal hanging around the jail. We plug the sheriff and we'll have him tracking us before morning—and he'd have plenty of help."

Nella nodded admiringly. "Can see you're still plenty smart," she said with a sly wink at Kissler. "I reckon it would be dumb to kill him—but put the handcuffs on him. We need to slow him down some."

"Aimed to do that, same as I'm going to spook his horse. He'll have to walk back to town—with them cuffs on."

Duke turned his attention to Ferd Kissler. "That make you happy, mister?" he asked in a sarcastic tone.

The tall man shrugged. "Sure does," he said, and

19

leaning over, pulled Seth Rossiter's arms into position behind his back. Then retrieving the manacles from the dust where he'd earlier dropped them, snapped them into place about the lawman's wrists and faced Duke. "That how you want it done, boss?" he asked dryly, tossing the ring of keys off into the weeds.

Duke nodded, unperturbed by the gambler's tone of voice. "Fine, just fine," he said, again taking Rossiter by the ankles. "Now, pick him up. I don't want him drug through the dirt."

A humorless smile cracked Kissler's thin lips but he said nothing. Lifting the lawman by the shoulders, he helped Finley carry him off into the brush.

Walking side by side, neither speaking, they doubled back to the road. When they reached the horses, Duke halted at Rossiter's bay, and slipping the bit, he gave the gelding a sharp crack on the hindquarters and sent him racing off into the grove at a hard gallop.

"That make you happy, too, mister?" Duke said to Kissler in the same ironic way.

The gambler's shoulders stirred. "Go to hell," he said softly, and headed off into the trees on the opposite side of the road, where he had left his mount.

Nella was waiting beside her horse. She ignored the friction between the two men, and handing a belted gun to Duke as he came up, she watched as he strapped on the weapon.

"Expect it feels good to be wearing a gun once more," she said.

"Does, for a fact," he replied, cinching the buckle. "Sure wished to hell we wasn't going to have that Ferd hanging around," he added, glancing in the direction that Kissler had disappeared. "Me and him's going to tangle, sure as shooting, before we get much older."

"Don't waste your time on him—he means nothing to me—or us," Nella said, and passed a handful of coins and several paper notes to the outlaw. "I figured you ought to have some cash in your pocket."

20

Duke grinned, thrust the money into his pants. Again impulsively reaching forward, he seized the woman by the shoulders, and pulling her close, kissed her once more.

"I just can't hardly wait!" he said in a husky voice. "I been dreaming of when you and me—"

"Somebody coming," Kissler warned from the edge of the road.

Finley released his grip on Nella, stepped back, and listened intently. He could hear nothing, and the suspicion that Ferd had made the statement merely to break up his moment with Nella entered his mind. But he let it pass. They had hung around too long, and the sooner they got on the move, the sooner they'd recover the money—and the sooner he'd be rid of the sonofabitch.

"Mount up," he said gruffly, still burning, nevertheless. "We got a long ways to go."

★ 5 ★

Head throbbing dully, shoulders cramping from the position in which he'd been left, Seth Rossiter heard the outlaws ride off. He had been vaguely aware of being carried from the road and dropped into the brush, of the low rumble of voices now and then, but nothing that was being spoken registered on his befuddled brain until the very last words.

He was fully conscious now, and a seething anger at his own stupidity and carelessness was surging through him. He had suspected—had actually felt within himself—that the woman lying in the road was a trap, an ambush. Why the hell hadn't he followed his instincts?

Scrambling a bit, Rossiter managed to get on his feet. The woman had been Rube Brodie's widow, he supposed. He'd heard of her, but had never seen her. And there was a man with her, a man who had hidden himself and his horse somewhere off the road and put in an appearance when Brodie's woman had locked her arms about him and jerked him off balance onto her.

His horse was gone. He'd heard Duke stampede the bay just before they departed, and he doubted there was any use in looking for the frightened animal. One good thing, he personally was unhurt except for the rap he'd taken on the head. It was hard to understand why they hadn't put a bullet into him and left him there, dead. He could thank Duke for that bit of soft-heartedness, he reckoned, or maybe it was the woman's idea to let him live.

Staggering as he walked, the lawman made his way back to the road. One thing he could count on, this whole thing was going to look to folks—just as U.S. Marshal Hill had said it would—like he had purposely allowed Duke Finley to escape. There'd be no convincing them otherwise and he guessed there was no point trying. The only way to clear himself of suspicion was to go after Duke and his two friends, fast, and recapture the outlaw.

And to do that meant returning to town as quickly as possible, getting another horse—assuming his own bay hadn't headed back to the settlement—and riding out at once after the outlaws. He was in for a bit of embarrassment, Rossiter knew, but he'd have to close his ears to what people would say when they saw him returning—afoot and handcuffed with his own irons. He'd have to swallow his pride and go on about the business of running down Duke Finley—which he fully intended to do, even if it took the rest of the year or longer.

On second thought, he reckoned it would be smart to bring in Jubal Seibert, have him along in case there was any tracking to be done. Jubal, although a bit cantankerous and hard to get along with, was an old army scout and one-time trapper in the high country roamed by Jim Bridger. Although well up in years now, he could still pick up a trail where almost none existed.

There was no sign of his horse as Seth, staying to the shoulder of the road where it was easier walking, began the ten-mile hike back to Cherryville. He still had his gun, which pleased him since it was one he'd carried for years and knew well. But he'd lost his hat somewhere in the brush and was too impatient to spend much time looking for it. However, in a short while he regretted leaving it behind; his head, bared to the hot sun and throbbing from the blow he had received, began to pain intensely. Since there was nothing he could do about it, the lawman bore it all stoically and trudged on.

He'd need a new outfit for the trail as well as another hat; blanket, slicker, a sack of coffee, and the means by which to make and drink it. He'd put Burt Antrum to work getting replacement gear and a horse ready while he sought out old Jubal and persuaded him to come along.

It was noon when he reached the outskirts of the settlement. His legs ached from the long walk in boots meant for riding, and his shoulders were a block of pain from their unaccustomed position. He was sweat-soaked, and his head was pounding insistently.

At once he angled to the left, thus avoiding the main street and the houses and business structures that stood along its length, and followed out the alley that ran behind the jail.

Despite his efforts, he nevertheless encountered a dozen or more townspeople, some of whom called out questions, while others simply stared at him in wonder—hatless, dusty, wrists locked behind his back—as he strode rigidly by. Chagrined, he only nodded and hurried on.

Finally he reached the rear of the jail and halted. Hoping that the deputy would be there, and that no one else would be present, he turned, backed up to the door, and tried the knob. The heavy panel was locked, as it should be. Angered, nevertheless, he pounded on it with a booted foot, determined that he'd not be forced to circle around the front of the structure, where he would be in full view of everyone abroad on the street.

Abruptly the door jerked open and Burt Antrum, face red, demanded, "What the hell you want banging on—" and then choked off when he saw who it was. As the lawman crowded past him into the jail, he added: "What happened, Sheriff? What're you doing back here and where's—"

"Get these damned cuffs off me!" Rossiter cut in harshly, and as the deputy hastily produced a key, the sheriff related what had occurred. "I got suckered good," he finished, rubbing his wrists and flexing his shoulders.

Antrum, a stockily built young man with a stubble of beard and a full mustache, stared at Rossiter in disbelief. That such a thing could take place seemed beyond his comprehension. After a moment he thrust his hands into the pockets of his denim pants and shook his head.

"They sure worked it slick," he murmured. Then, as if to console the lawman, he added, "Took some mighty smart doing to outfox you, Sheriff. . . . You bleeding some?"

Rossiter had turned, was obtaining another hat from the row of pegs on the wall. "Not enough to bother with—and this song's not over yet. I'm going after them soon as I can get set."

Antrum frowned, rubbed at his neck. "You think that's a good idea, Sheriff? You been hurt and you've had a mighty long walk. Expect you ought to sort of take it easy. Now, I know I ain't nowheres as good a lawman as you, but I can take out after them if you want—"

Rossiter cut in quickly, "No, I lost Duke and I'll get him back—along with that pair who helped him. Obliged to you, though."

The deputy continued to scrub at the back of his neck. He wore a fancy tooled Mexican belt and holster, which was in strange contrast to the dirty sleeves of the underwear visible below the cuffs of his faded blue shirt.

"Maybe I best ride along with you, Sheriff, there

being three of them now and you . . . well . . . you not being in such good shape."

"I'll do fine," Rossiter said. "Now, I want you to go over to the livery stable, get me another horse. I'll be needing the same gear as you put on my bay. I'm in a hell of a hurry so don't diddle around any."

Antrum nodded. "Yes sir. Where'll you be?"

"Probably here by the time you get back with something for me to ride. Right now, I'm going over after Seibert. Want to take him along in case I need some tracking done."

"That's a good idea," the deputy said, and pivoting, hurried off through the open doorway and struck off down the street for the livery stable.

Rossiter found Jubal Seibert sitting on the porch of his shack at the edge of town, whetting the already razor-sharp edge of his skinning knife. The old man, still favoring a fringed deerskin shirt and moccasins, along with a worn pair of army pants and ragged-brimmed cavalry hat, looked up as the lawman approached.

"Set a bit," he greeted, motioning to an old rocking chair over which was thrown a soft buffalo hide. "Was tuning up to go hunting. You of a mind to come along? Seen a young doe about a mile—"

"Can't make it this time, Jubal," Rossiter said. "Fact is, I've come looking to you for help."

The rhythmic whisp-whisp-whisp of steel against the oil stone stopped as Seibert ceased his whetting. "How so?"

Seth Rossiter brushed at the sweat on his face and supplied a frank account of what had occurred earlier on the road, sparing none of the details regardless of how embarrassing. When he had finished, the old scout hawked, spat.

"Reckon that'll learn you to pay a mind to your common sense. Surprises me some, Seth, you not listening."

26

"I knew better," the lawman admitted, "but I acted like some greenhorn."

"You sure did. . . . What do you want me for?"

"I'm taking out after Duke and his friends soon as Antrum gets me a horse ready. They'll be going after the money, I figure, and being about a day behind them, like I will be, there could be some tracking will have to be done. Like for you to be along in case there is."

Jubal Seibert scrubbed at his tobacco-stained beard, stared off toward the hills to the west. "Well, I ain't looking to work none, my bones not being what they once was—"

"Pay'll be a dollar a day and found, same as always."

"Ain't enough but I reckon it's fair. Anyways, it ain't the getting paid that's making me say yes, it's that you're needing a favor and someday it could be on the other foot." Seibert rose, slid the knife into its well-oiled belt scabbard. "You're wanting to pull out right soon, I take it—"

"Quick as my horse is ready. Can you leave now?"

"Sure—just have to get my horse. You go on back to your jail, I'll be there shortly."

Rossiter bucked his head in approval. "Fine," he said as he turned away, and then pausing, added: "I'm obliged to you, Jubal, for siding me."

"Ain't nothing," the old scout said with a wave of his hand. "I reckon that deer'll still be there when I get back."

★ 6 ★

"Can we make this Cougar Ridge by dark?" Ferd Kissler asked when they slowed the horses to a walk.

They had ridden hard and fast since the incident with Sheriff Rossiter, wanting to put as much distance between them as possible before he could recover, return to Cherryville, and mount a posse.

Duke laughed, winked at Nella. "You don't know nothing about this country, do you, mister?"

"Damn little," Ferd said easily, rubbing the jade pendant idly between a thumb and forefinger. "Spent my time mostly over Kansas and Nebraska way."

"We'll probably get to Cougar Ridge tomorrow afternoon," Nella said, bridging the enmity that simmered between the two men. "We'll camp out tonight."

Finley grinned broadly at Kissler. "Dude, you reckon you can stand a night out in the woods with the varmints?"

Ferd made no reply, choosing to ignore the question.

Nella swiped impatiently at the beads of sweat gathered on her cheeks, shook her head irritably. "There's no sense in the two of you snapping at each other like you've been doing," she said. "I don't know how long we're going to be together, since I don't

28

know where the money is, but it'll make things a heap easier for all if you'll try to get along."

"Yes, ma'am, sure," Duke said, laughing. "Hell, I can get along with a polecat if I have to."

Kissler stirred on his saddle, let the nugget of jade fall free. Nella glanced at him and then to Duke. Suddenly anxious to get away from what was an explosive situation, she lifted her reins and looked ahead.

"Hadn't we better hurry it along a bit? The horses have caught their wind—"

"I don't figure there's any great big need," Duke said. "That sheriff'll have to walk clean back to town."

"Unless somebody happens along and gives him a ride," Kissler said.

"Now, that ain't likely!" Duke countered. "You seen anybody on this road? Hell, no you ain't—and you won't! Only folks that ever use it are them that lives over here on this side of the mountains. I know, because I growed up around here."

Kissler shrugged. "All right, nobody'll come along, but it still won't take that sheriff all day to get back to town. And it won't take long to get a posse together and head out after us, either—"

"*If* he gets hisself a posse," Duke cut in. "Been thinking about that. Sort of figured at first that was what Seth would do, but I've been hashing it around in my head and I ain't so sure. I've known him for a-plenty of years, and he's mighty proud. Just could be he'll saddle up another horse and light out after us all alone."

"Which means he'll be on our tails all the sooner— not taking time to get a posse together," Ferd said, and swore deeply. "I should've put a bullet in his head back there like I wanted. There'd be no fretting over him now."

"Seems you'd rather worry about a U.S. Marshal and a posse and about half the lawmen in the territory chasing us. That it?"

"Nope, and for sure they'd not be on us today, or even tomorrow—it all depending on when somebody found the body. Hell, we might even had us a week—and that'd give us plenty of time to dig up the money and get clean out of the country before they started hunting for you."

"Me? Don't go forgetting you're in this right up to your hatband!"

"Who's to say I am?" Ferd said with a smile. "Same goes for Nella. Nobody seen us excepting that sheriff, and he would've been dead. You're the jasper they'd all be looking for, because you were the one he was taking to the pen—and the only one with him."

Duke gave that thought. Then, "Well, there's no sense chawing it over—it's done. And I figure I was right in keeping you from shooting Rossiter and I'll stand by it. Way I see it, we've got nothing to worry about, anyway. Coming down the road with him, I done plenty of talking, made Rossiter think that if I had the chance I'd head for Mexico. That's where he'll figure I've gone. Could be I'll do it, too, when I get my money—"

Kissler cut in. "*Our* money. Best you remember that Nella and me's got a claim on it, too."

"Nella, maybe, but you sure and hell ain't!" Duke stated, bristling. "All you got coming is what she said she'd give you for helping."

The gambler's jaw hardened and a reply formed on his thin lips. Then, as if thinking better of it, he remained silent.

"You don't think we need to keep hurrying?" Nella asked, returning to her earlier question. "I'm not so sure that it's safe to take our time."

"I am," Duke said flatly. "I know Seth Rossiter and I know this here country. Still, I reckon it won't hurt none to sort of get right along until dark, or maybe even later'n that—say, midnight.

"Then we can camp till morning and head out for

Cougar Ridge soon as it's light. Ought to get us there by noon, doing it that way. Can lay over there, have us a good restaurant meal, and sleep in the Cattleman Hotel. There's a good saloon right next door to it, Ferd, where you can have yourself a real good time. Me and Nella's going to be busy. We got us a lot of catching up to do."

Kissler gave the woman a covert glance. Unnoticed by Duke, she shook her head slightly.

"Me and Rube stayed at the Cattleman once," Finley continued. "Sure is a fine place. I'll bet you'll like it, Nella—big soft beds, carpets on the floor, nice settin' chairs. They got real fancy lace curtains on the windows, and the shades are them slick rolling kind that you pull down and they'll wind back up."

"Seems I remember Rube telling me about that place," Nella said. "Don't you think it'd be smarter to pass up the town and keep riding, in case that sheriff does get on our trail faster'n we figure?"

"And what about a telegraph?" Ferd said. "Ain't there a chance that he could send a message to the law in this Cougar Springs and have him waiting for us?"

"Showing your ignorance again, dude," Finley said, wagging his head. "There ain't no telegraph on this side of the mountains. Only way you can get word to anywheres along here is a letter on the stagecoach— and it don't go through but once a week—or maybe I best say once in two weeks, 'cause it goes north one week, south the next. Nope, we won't be taking no chance putting up at the Cattleman for a night."

"We best keep going," Ferd said stubbornly. "Sooner get to that—"

"Dammit, I already told you once, and I ain't figuring to do it again—you ain't got nothing to say about anything!" Duke shouted. "You're the hired help and you best start remembering it! If me and Nella wants to spend a night in the hotel catching up, then that sure'n hell's what we'll do! Ain't that right, Nella?"

Rube Brodie's widow looked straight ahead. After several moments Duke kneed his mount in closer to hers. Leaning over he studied her closely.

"I said, 'Ain't that right, Nella'?"

She turned to him, a pleading sort of expression in her eyes. "There's nothing I'd like better, Duke, but I'm afraid! I guess it's because of Rube—of losing him, I mean—and I have to play everything safe."

"You saying you don't want to spend the night in Cougar Ridge like me?"

She nodded, smiled hopefully at him. "Please, Duke—kind of do things my way, will you? I'm sure you're right about that sheriff not catching up with us, but I worry about it—about things like that. I don't have the heart to take chances anymore."

"She's right about not stopping," Ferd observed. "You—"

"Shut up, damn you!" Finley cut in savagely. "This here's between me and my woman—"

"Your woman? Since when did—"

"Since me and Rube started running together, and that's a long time before anybody even heard of you! Me and Nella's always been soft on each other but we wasn't about to double-cross old Rube. Now, mister, if you don't think that's the how of it between me and her, why you just—"

"If we get to Cougar Ridge around noon tomorrow, look how much farther we could go before dark!" Nella said hurriedly. "Then I could forget worrying about that sheriff and a posse. Duke, please go along with me on this—just this one time?"

Finley squirmed on his saddle, sleeved away the sweat on his face. "Well, sure, if that's what you're a-wanting so bad. But it's a mighty big disappointment to me. I been looking toward being with you ever since we hatched up this deal."

"Another night won't make any difference—"

"No, maybe it won't. Next town we'll be coming to

after Cougar Ridge'll be Pine Valley. It ain't got no real fine hotel but there's a place we can go—"

"It'll be fine," Nella said. "We won't be too far from where you hid the money, once we're there, will we?"

At Nella's question, Ferd Kissler half turned, considered Duke expectantly, thumb and forefinger again caressing the jade nugget.

"Nope, but we won't be close, neither," Duke said, his manner dejected. "I'll let you know when we get there. . . . Come on, since you're so all fired set on not stopping at Cougar Ridge. We might as well cover all the miles we can," he added, and drumming on the sides of his horse with his heels, put the gray gelding into a fast lope.

★ 7 ★

"Here's the place," Rossiter said, pulling his horse to a stop.

Jubal Seibert dropped from the saddle to the loose dust in the road and padded silently on his moccasin-shod feet to the spot the lawman had indicated. Squatting, he studied the scuffed area.

"Yep, reckon this'll be it. Can see where the woman was laying. Then you come from over there, I reckon," he said, pointing off to the right.

Rossiter nodded impatiently. "That's how it was. And the man who clubbed me must've been waiting on the other side of the road—but I don't give a damn about that now. What I want to know for sure is which way did they head when they rode off? It sounded like they went north—but I've got to be dead certain."

Jubal drew himself upright, spat, and after again scrutinizing the immediate area carefully, moved off a short distance along the road. Moments later he halted, once more dropped to his haunches for a close inspection of the dust, and then rose.

"North, all right," he said, returning to where the lawman waited. "Leastwise, that's how they went from here."

"Not south, for the border?"

"Nope, sign's right there, plain as day," Seibert replied peevishly. "Three horses, one with a real worn-off shoe. Heading north. What's got you thinking they might've lit out for Mexico?"

"Duke. He was talking big about where he'd go if he got the chance. I reckon that's all it was—big talk aimed at throwing me off." Rossiter paused as Jubal Seibert swung stiffly back onto his saddle, and then together they moved off along the road. "He was laying the groundwork for what was coming."

Jubal did not look up. His dark, old eyes, narrowed to cut down the glare, were fixed on the dusty ribbon ahead of them. "You're a-figuring he had this all schemed up?"

"I'm sure of it," the lawman said. "He somehow got in touch with Brodie's widow and together they set up the whole thing. It went off without a hitch—proving it was all planned."

"And you're for sure who she is, too? I recollect you saying there was a woman but you wasn't dead certain who she was."

"Had to be her. Duke didn't have a wife, and he never hung around a woman long enough to get cozy with her. It was always one night, two at the most, and then he'd pull out."

Jubal nodded, and then said, "Expect we can put these horses to loping now. Them tracks just keep on going north. They ain't doubling back."

Rossiter, relieved, raked his mount with spurs, and as Jubal followed suit, both animals broke into a brisk gallop.

Veering in closer to the lawman in order to make conversation a bit easier, Seibert said: "Reckon what she's after is her half of that money Duke and her man cached."

"That would be it," Rossiter replied, raising his

voice to be heard. "Probably been planning this for weeks."

"She ever come see him while he was in your jail?"

"No, never did."

"Far as you know—"

The lawman nodded. "Yeh, far as I know, but I figure I would. Pretty sure Antrum would've told me if she'd come around while I was gone—and at night, with the jail all locked up, there's no way she could've got in to see him. She couldn't even get near enough to talk."

"Well," Seibert said, "she sure had to fix things up with him somehow. Duke had to know she'd be waiting along the road, on the right day, for him."

Rossiter grinned ruefully. "No matter how or what, they pulled it off and I was left holding the bag—one I sure aim to fill, fast."

"I reckon that depends on how far Duke's got to go to get the money. Farther it is, better chance we've got of catching up. Ain't you got no idea a'tall where him and Brodie stashed it?"

Rossiter shook his head. "None. Good bet it's on this side of the mountains—and somewhere between Capital City and Cherryville."

"Covers one hell of a lot of territory," the old man said. "One thing for certain, we're going to have to keep an eye on them tracks. They just maybe'll turn off the road somewheres. And should we come to a rocky mesa or a gravel flat, we might lose them."

Rossiter said, "Just why I got you to come along. I plain can't afford to lose them."

Jubal Seibert fell silent for a long minute, and then said, "Well, I aim to do my best, Sheriff—and I reckon that's all a mule can do."

They were moving steadily along the well-defined road through a grove of cottonwoods, brush, and mounds of reddish soil. But that would end soon, Rossiter knew, and the cool comfort of the trees would drop behind and they would come out into a broken land of chaparral, mesquite, needle-sharp yucca, and snakeweed. And it would be so until they reached the next settlement, Cougar Ridge, which lay at the foot of the towering Sacramento Peaks.

"You ain't got no idea either who that jasper was that whomped you over the head?" Jubal said after a time.

"Never got even a glimpse of him. He came up on me from behind, and the woman had her arms around me, was pulling me down. Was fixed to where I could hardly move."

"Probably some bird Brodie's widow took up with—maybe even married up to."

"Likely. I don't think she'd hire on somebody to help—not when she was planning to hook up with Duke—and that's what she'd have to do if she wanted some of the money. Rube didn't live long enough to tell her or get word to her where the money was stashed. Only Duke knows the spot, so she had to line up with him."

Jubal had raised himself in his stirrups and was looking ahead. They were well out of the trees now and were climbing a long slope toward a pass that cut a narrow gash in the horizon above them.

Turning his head, the scout spat, faced the lawman. "That ground's got mighty hard—and I ain't seeing no tracks. But they for sure started up the hill for the pass. And there ain't no reason for them to be turning off along here."

Rossiter's glance swept the deserted land to either side, and he shrugged. "No, but we best find that trail again, once we top out, just to be sure."

"Aim to," Jubal said laconically.

The horses had dropped back to a walk on the fairly steep grade, and by the time they reached the pass, the animals were plastered with sweat. Rossiter and the scout rode on through the cut, no more than a wagon's length in width, and drew to a halt on its far side. Immediately, Seibert slid from his saddle and began a close inspection of the hard, rock-studded soil.

After a few moments he straightened up, looked off across the endless sage-green and brown flat unrolling before them. "They was here, all right," he said. "And they're still headed north."

Rossiter grunted his satisfaction, and twisting about, glanced to the west. The day was growing late. In another hour the sun would be gone. Coming back around, he searched the far-reaching country ahead with narrowed eyes.

"Can see a clump of green up there a ways. Could mean water," he said, pointing. "When we come to there, we might as well pull up for the night. Horses are starting to show wear."

"Just what I was hoping you'd say," Seibert said, going back onto his saddle. "Ain't no sense running them into the ground trying to catch up with that bunch the first day. We keep at it, and they stay out in front, we'll be on their tails plenty soon enough."

Rossiter mopped at his face with a bandanna. "Could be that'll happen pretty soon. I know Duke, and him being cooped up like he's been, he'll want to do some celebrating at the first saloon he comes to—and that'll be Cougar Ridge."

"Expect you're right," Jubal agreed. "We get us a early start in the morning—just maybe this here chasing'll be all over by dark."

★ 8 ★

Despite steady riding, it was late in the afternoon when the lawman and Jubal Seibert reached Cougar Ridge. Halting at the end of the single main street, Rossiter pointed to a two-story square building standing near the center of the settlement. Painted a bright yellow, with brown doors and window trim, it was a garish splash in the slanting sunlight.

"That's the hotel," he said. "Owner calls it the Cattleman."

"Sort of big for this place, ain't it?"

"Gets most of its business from pilgrims using the crossroad coming from the east and going west. Kind of a favorite with ranchers, too—having a good saloon and casino.

"You figure Duke'll still be here?"

The lawman brushed at his chin, rubbed the stubble of sweat-soaked whiskers. "He always liked to hang around a place like the Cattleman, so he could be. Expect it all depends on how anxious he is to get to that money."

"I reckon we better hope he is," Seibert said. "Way we been pushing these horses, they won't be good for many more days of it."

Rossiter turned, glanced at the old army scout, a puzzled look in his eyes. To his way of thinking, they had not worked their mounts hard at all, and both were in fine shape. It was all a matter of opinion, he guessed.

"And him staying overnight, he'll still have a day's start on us—maybe more."

Rossiter nodded, put his attention back onto the street, all but deserted at that near-supper hour.

"He'll have that much lead for sure, but Duke would have a hard time passing up a saloon like the one here—after being in jail all that time. We maybe'll be lucky. Let's work around to the back and come in from there."

Jubal clucked to the buckskin he was riding, and followed the lawman as he circled the structures lined along the street and moved in behind the hotel. As they halted at the long hitchrack placed in the shade of several large oak trees, he critically eyed the horses waiting there.

"Ain't none of them animals been rode for hours. You know what kind of a horse Duke was forking?"

"A gray—if he's still on the one I got for him from the livery stable in Cherryville."

"No gray in that bunch," Seibert said. "Reckon I'll have me a look-see in the hotel's barn. Maybe find it there."

Before he finished speaking, he was off his saddle and shambling toward the low-roofed building set back in another cluster of trees. Rossiter rode the remaining short distance to the rack, dismounted, and tying his horse to the crossbar, dropped back, caught up the reins of Seibert's buckskin, and secured him also. As he finished, the scout emerged from the stables and rejoined him.

"No gray in there," he said, rubbing at his thighs. "Truth is, there ain't no horses in there a'tall. Place is plumb empty. Business must be mighty scarce!"

Seth Rossiter shrugged. "Always better at night. You talk to the hostler?"

"Weren't around. Weren't nobody around."

The lawman pulled off his hat, ran long fingers through his damp hair. Stable help was generally a good source of information concerning travelers, a livery barn being the place where they left their animals for care and feeding.

"Probably find him in the casino—or maybe he's gone home to supper," Rossiter said. "Let's go have a few words with the bartender."

With Seibert at his shoulder, he crossed the hard-pack lying between the hitchrack and the rear of the building. Reaching there, he opened the door, and led the way into the cool, half-dark interior of the saloon.

The bartender appeared little better off for business than the stableman. There was one customer at the end of the long counter, while three men sat at a corner table in conversation with a saloon girl.

Crossing to the bar, Rossiter ordered whiskey, while Jubal Seibert spoke for beer. When the drinks were served, the sheriff laid a coin on the counter—held it there with the tip of a finger pressing it down. The bartender, reaching for it, withdrew his hand, stared at the lawman woodenly.

"Looking for a man I know," Rossiter said. "Used to hang around here—I think he might've lived somewhere close by."

The saloonkeeper shrugged. "He got a name?"

"Finley—Duke Finley. Likely was with a woman and another man."

The bartender shook his head, but there was a reserve visible in his small eyes. "Nope, I ain't seen him."

Rossiter's jaw hardened. It was obvious to him that the man was lying. "Think about it again," he said in a tight voice. "It's important I find him."

The bartender's glance brushed the star on Seth

Rossiter's vest, drifted on to stare toward the front of the saloon and the empty street beyond the swinging-door entrance. The girl with the three cowhands laughed suddenly, her voice high-pitched.

"I'm telling you I ain't seen Du . . . him—"

Rossiter drew back, considered the man coldly. Drawing his pistol, he held it loosely in his hand while he surveyed the ornate mirror of the backbar and the bottle-and-glass-loaded shelves that fronted it.

"You reckon a little target practice'd refresh your memory, mister?" he asked softly.

The saloonman's mouth tightened and a look of uncertainty flooded into his eyes. "Hell—you ain't going to do nothing like that! You're a lawman and you can't. Anyways, I'll holler for the town marshal—"

"Go ahead. Like as not he's a friend of mine. But whether he is or not won't make any difference. You're interfering with the law—holding back real important information. He'll side with me . . . Jubal, you like to make a little bet?"

The scout brushed at his mustache, wiping away the flecks of beer foam, and grinned. "Sure. What're we betting on?"

"Well, I'm a mite out of practice but I've got a silver dollar that says I can hit the middle of that rose at the top of the mirror."

"I'm taking that bet," Seibert said, pulling his own weapon—a long-barreled cap and ball Colt that had been converted to use cartridges. "If you miss, I'll just try my hand—only I sort of favor that there little angel to the right of your rose. I figure I can lop off its head first time."

"All right—have at it. I'll wait till—"

"Hold off!" the bartender yelled suddenly as Jubal raised his arm and leveled his pistol. "Duke was here, like you figured. Him and them others."

Rossiter gave that brief thought, cocked the hammer

of his weapon, and idly sighted on the rose he had chosen as his target. "They put up here for the night?"

"Nope—no, sir," the bartender replied nervously. "Stuck around for a spell—four, maybe five hours, I reckon it was, resting and drinking—taking it easy. What's Duke gone and done this time?"

"Got hisself crossways of the law," Seibert said. "They say where they was headed?"

The bartender hesitated, glanced about. The old scout again lifted his heavy weapon, squinted down the barrel at the cherub selected by him for devastation.

"Hell, he didn't tell me! Seemed sort of put out with them two others. Was having an argument, I think."

"You know over what?"

"Ain't for sure, but I think it was about staying the night here at the hotel. Whoever it was wanting to go on—the woman, I think—must've won out 'cause that's what they done."

"Which way?" Jubal repeated. "You ain't said yet."

The cowhands and the girl had become aware of the somewhat tense discussion at the bar and were now giving it their undivided attention. The solitary customer who had been present at the bar when Rossiter and Jubal arrived had disappeared.

"North—anyways, that's the road they took," the bartender said in a ragged voice.

"You for damn sure it wasn't east—for Texas?" Rossiter demanded.

"Yes, sir—was north. I seen them ride out."

"All three of them?"

"All three—"

Rossiter motioned for a refill of his glass. "You catch the name of the woman and the other man?"

"Yeh, reckon I did. Duke done some introducing," the saloonman said, replenishing both glasses. "Woman's name was Brodie—Nella Brodie. Used to be the wife of a friend of his'n."

43

He'd been right about the woman, the lawman realized. "And the man?"

"Called him Ferd Kissler. Looked like a gambler to me. Had them blank kind of eyes."

"You ever seen him around here before?"

"Nope, never have. Pure stranger."

Kissler was a newcomer to him, too, Rossiter thought, and stepped back. "Obliged to you for the information. Whatever's left over from that dollar after you take out for the drinks, stick it in your pocket. We'll be spending the night, so if you think of anything else, speak up."

Seibert glanced at the lawman, relief in his expression. "Sure glad to hear you say that! Was a-feared you'd be wanting to go on, and them horses of ours—"

"Expect they can use the rest," Rossiter said dryly as they turned away. "You see to stabling them, while I get us fixed up with a room."

"Sure enough," the scout said, and pausing, laid a hand on Seth Rossiter's shoulder. "Just one thing afore I forget—get that danged star you're wearing out of sight! It'll make getting answers to questions a lot easier if the jasper you're talking to don't know you're the law!"

Rossiter smiled. "Reckon I forgot," he said, and unpinning the badge, dropped it into his shirt pocket as he entered the hotel's lobby.

★ 9 ★

"There ain't nobody following us," Duke said as he and his two companions rode steadily north. "We could've stayed in Cougar Ridge like I wanted."

Nella Brodie smiled patiently. "We can't be sure, Duke, just because we don't see anybody."

Finley shifted on his saddle. "Well, next time we're doing what I say. This here's my party and, by God, I'm calling the shots!"

"The money's half Nella's," Ferd observed in his quiet, dry way. "That gives her a say-so."

"It don't give nobody nothing unless I take them to where I cached that money—and I'm the only one that can," Finley snapped, and then narrowing his eyes, pointed at the pendant hanging outside Kissler's shirt. "Been aiming to ask, what's that there green thingamajig you've got around your neck? Where I come from, only womenfolk wears necklaces."

"It's jade—a good-luck charm. Got it down in Mexico."

"It ever do you any good?"

"Plenty of times," Kissler said, and smiled at the woman.

45

Duke hawked, spat to show his contempt for such nonsense. Patting the pistol on his hip, he said, "This here's the only kind of good-luck piece I got any use for. Works every time, too. . . . Now, suppose you just ride on ahead a way. I got some real private talking to do with Nella—and getting private with her sure ain't nothing a man can do with you sticking around close as crows at a corn husking."

Kissler threw a quick glance at Nella, shrugged, and then spurring his horse, moved forward a dozen yards. Duke swung in nearer to the woman, scrubbed away the sweat clinging to his whisker stubble, and grinned.

"It'll sure be real good when that jasper's gone! How much did you promise to pay him?"

"Twenty-five hundred dollars," Nella replied.

Duke whistled softly. "That's a hell of a lot of money for doing a favor!"

"Was several, not just one. And they were important—big—like I've explained to you. Rube left me flat busted. Ferd came up with cash when I had to have it." She paused, looked ahead. They were taking it easy, the horses moving at a slow trot. "Owe that deputy, too."

Duke swore again, then scratched at his beard. "Deputy? What deputy?"

"One back at the jail in Cherryville—Antrum I think his name is."

"What in the hell do you owe him for?"

Nella sighed, continued to stare out across the flat they were crossing. There was little to be seen except the glittering sand, yucca plants, gaunt cholla cactus, and an occasional water-starved cedar. But far in the distance a shadowy blue-gray range of mountains loomed, promising eventual relief from the bleakness through which they were passing.

"It was for smuggling all those notes about our plans into you, and how I intended to get you away from

46

that sheriff when he started for the pen with you. You had to know what to expect.

"You think Antrum did all that just because I smiled at him? There was a time when that would have worked, but it was long ago."

"Ain't been that long, Nell," Duke said, employing the affectionate diminutive that he'd heard Rube use on occasions. "Far as I'm concerned, you're still one hell of a fine-looking woman, and far as I'm concerned your smile'll buy the town! You know, I done a lot of remembering while I was locked up—and planning."

"Planning? Before you heard from me?"

"Yeh. Made up my mind they'd never get me to the pen—even if I had to kill whoever it was taking me there."

"Thought you and that sheriff was real close chums—"

"We was—once. But I didn't figure on it being him taking me. I figured it would be the deputy or maybe that U.S. marshall—Hill. I aimed to watch my chances, catch whoever it was not looking, and bust in his skull with a rock or maybe a club."

"But you wouldn't've done it if it had been that sheriff—"

Duke stirred on the saddle, studied half a dozen vultures circling high above something well to the right of the road. "I just ain't sure what I would've done," he said finally. "I'd got away, for sure, but I wouldn't've killed old Seth. Expect I'd'a tried talking him into throwing in with me, getting the money and then skedaddling across the border with it."

"That was before you heard from me—"

"Yep. Up to that time Antrum passed me your letter I didn't know what had become of you."

"You probably figured I was dead—"

"Or married up to some jaybird and moved out of the country. I'm sure glad that wasn't the way of it, Nella! You know how I always felt about you, but I just couldn't ever let myself go on account of you belonging to Rube. But after I heard from you—and Rube being out of it—I started in making real big plans for us."

For a long minute the only sounds were the dry creak of saddle leather, the thud of the horses' hoofs. Then, in a faint voice, Nella said, "I see—"

Duke's eyes filled with concern, then anger. "What's the matter? It don't much look like you go for the idea."

"It's—it's sort of unexpected."

"Hell's afire, Nella, it's only natural for it to be me and you now that Rube's dead. Always wanted you for my woman, and now with all that money just waiting for us, we got the chance to eat high on the hog for the rest of our lives!

"I figure we can turn around and head right back for the border when we get the money. I know a place down-river from El Paso where there ain't no soldiers or nobody else hanging around to ask questions. We can cross over there and head straight for Chihuahua.

"Folks can live like kings and queens down there if they've got money—and we'll sure have a-plenty. Can have us a *hacienda*, with Mex servants waiting on us hand and foot, and all we'll have to do is lay around and enjoy ourselves."

"I had some plans of my own," Nella said haltingly, choosing her words with care. "There's a few things I'd like to do with my share—my half."

"Meaning your plans don't figure on me?" Duke asked, his voice rising sharply.

She turned to him, gestured helplessly. "Well, I didn't know what you aimed to do. I thought you probably had plans, too—same as I did."

Finley's eyes were again on the vultures. They had tightened their circle of flight and were beginning to drop lower. Whatever it was they were watching—an animal, or possibly a man—had reached death or was very near to it.

"Naw, this here's all wrong—we're better off tying up together," Duke said, shifting his gaze to Ferd, who had twisted about and was looking back, wondering, no doubt, if the conversation to which he was not privileged had come to an end. "Together we got thirty thousand dollars, more or less, once we get those yahoos you're owing paid off. We split up, and we only got half that much apiece."

"I realize that, Duke, but fifteen thousand dollars is not to be sneezed at! When you come right down to it, it's a lot of money!"

"But fifteen thousand ain't thirty thousand and that's what it's going to be if we do like I want. Just what kind of plans have you got that's so much better'n mine, anyway?"

"Thought I'd take a trip, go back East, see some of the big cities. Always wanted to do that. And then I'd like to buy myself a little business somewhere out here."

"You ain't scheming something up with that Ferd Kissler, are you?" Duke demanded suddenly. "Sometimes he acts pretty much like he owns you."

"Well, he don't!" Nella snapped, dabbing at her face with a handkerchief. "Nobody does, and that includes—" She broke off abruptly as if deciding not to complete the thought. "Ferd is only a man who helped me when I needed help—he was dealing blackjack in a saloon where I was working. He's nothing more than a friend."

"Well, he sure better mind his crupper or me and him's going to tangle. I plain don't like him making out he's so much when he pure ain't nothing, far as I'm concerned. Fact is, this whole danged thing's sort of simmering down to nothing. If you ain't figuring to throw in with me, why, there ain't nothing for me to look ahead to."

"But you could go on to Mexico yourself—"

"Nope, not without you. If you ain't willing to do like I want—take the whole thirty thousand and tie up with me—then I'd just as soon forget about the money, let it stay right where it is."

★ 10 ★

"These here horses ain't going to make it to the next town if we don't let up on them a mite," Jubal Seibert said disapprovingly. "We're pushing them too danged hard."

Rossiter's set features relaxed slightly as he slowed down the sorrel he was riding. Being the one who established the pace, he hadn't realized they had been moving at a good lope for some time.

"Wasn't thinking," he replied, lifting his voice to be heard above the drumming hoofs. "Got my mind so fixed on catching up with that bunch that I forget everything else."

Jubal reached down, rubbed the sweaty neck of his buckskin. "I ain't telling you how to run your business, but could be we've got a far piece to go afore this'll be over, so we best go a mite easy. This ain't no country to get caught on foot."

"No doubt, but we're not hurting them any," Rossiter replied in a curt voice. "Maybe it's you."

Jubal's thin shoulders stirred, and pulling off his old campaign hat, he ran his fingers through his graying hair.

"Sorry I said that," Rossiter added. "Didn't mean it exactly the way it sounded."

Seibert had replaced the hat and was now slumped forward on his saddle. Digging into a side pocket, he procured a plug of near-black tobacco, bit off a chew after offering it to the lawman, who refused, and returned it to its place.

"I reckon, you taking it so hard, Duke's the first prisoner you ever lost."

"First one," Seth admitted. "But that's not it. Expect I'd look at it a bit different if it was somebody besides Duke Finley."

"Him being a friend of yours once—is that what's eating at you?"

The lawman nodded. "Folks know that—know that we were plenty close for a lot of years before I pinned on a star."

"So? Can't see where that cuts any hay."

"Does—a-plenty. J. W. Hill, the U.S. marshal, made me see that. Mentioned that people will think I let Duke get away on account of us being such good friends once. Some might even figure that Duke cut me in on the money, paid me off to let him escape."

"Well, what folks think and what you knows is the truth can be two mighty different things."

"I know that, but you'll have to admit that it'll look like there's something to the idea—me turning down Hill's offer to ride with me, and then falling for that woman's trick the way I did. Hell, a greenhorn deputy constable would've known better!"

"Maybe. All depends, I reckon, on how a man's been brought up. You're the kind that when you see a woman you figure's in trouble, you just naturally got to help. Plenty other men would've left her laying there right where she was, thinking maybe it was a trick, or else just plain not wanting to get mixed up in anything."

"I was careful—went at it slow. Still got tricked—"

"You got no call to go faulting yourself. You done what you thought was right and needful!"

Rossiter shook his head. "Can't agree with you, Jubal," he said, mopping at the sweat on his forehead. "No excuse for any lawman to lose a prisoner. He should be smart enough to keep it from happening."

"Which brings us right back to the beginning, I reckon, and there sure ain't no sense in arguing in a circle. Man never gets nowhere doing it."

"Except it puts us right back to what I said at the start. I've got to catch Duke, no matter what or how long it takes."

Jubal clucked, spat a stream of tobacco juice off onto a roadside rock. "Well, my head ain't hanging sideways from too much brains, but it sure seems to me you're taking this a mite too hard. You'll catch that bird—you'll lay him by the heels sooner or later."

"Can't wait for later," Rossiter said, glancing about. "You figure we're making up time on them?"

"Can bet on it. I misdoubt they're riding hard as we are. . . . What's the next town we're coming to?"

"Pine Valley."

"We be getting there tomorrow?"

"Yeh—and we could make it by morning if we rode all night."

Jubal Seibert swore, spat again. "Now, that would be a dang fool thing to do, Sheriff, and you know it! If we was to do that, and then they wasn't there, we'd find ourselves setting on our backsides with a couple of plumb wore-out horses that couldn't be straddled for a whole day—and we'd for sure get left behind! You ain't thinking about doing that, are you?" the old scout added in a concerned voice.

"If the odds were good that they'd be there when we rode in, I would—"

"But the odds all run in the other direction," Jubal said. "Way I see it, we're just going to have to plug along steady-like, and pretty soon we'll catch up. . . ."

This Pine Valley town, it in them mountains to the north?"

Rossiter nodded, and taking up his canteen, removed the cork and had a swallow of the tepid water. "Not much of a place," he said, lowering the container after restoring its cap and hanging it on the saddlehorn once more. "Can't see Duke laying over there if he'd pass up a town like Cougar Ridge. I'm not even sure they've got a hotel in Pine Valley."

"Could be he's hurrying right along so's he can get to that cached money—figuring that you'd be on his trail quick as you could get yourself another horse—and then keep on going, maybe even aiming to leave the country."

The lawman smiled, nodded. "You're starting to get the idea, Jubal—the reason why I'm in such a rush. There's no time to lose, far as I'm concerned. Duke could make it to the stash, pick it up, and keep right on going. What I've got to hope for is that he'll pull up somewhere along the way and give me the chance to overtake him."

"Well, for dang sure he's got to rest his horse and them the woman and the other fellow are riding, same as we do. An animal can only do so much, and in this here heat, and that up-and-down country we're heading into, a man's got to expect even less from them. . . . We better be thinking about pulling up for the night pretty soon."

Rossiter glanced to the sun. It was dropping rapidly and would soon be gone below the ragged silhouette of hills in the west. He came back around, looked ahead.

"We'll keep going till full dark. No place in sight worth making a camp, anyway. It'll have to be out on the flat."

Seibert pulled at his beard, spat another stream of tobacco juice. "Won't be the first time. . . . You got some of that grain left in your saddlebags? Horse of mine can use a bait."

"Be glad to split what's left between him and the sorrel. Can get more when we stop at Pine Valley. Best we water them, too. Can refill the canteens tomorrow."

Jubal, partly standing in his stirrups as he scanned the landscape for a place to make night camp, finally gave it up, concluding, apparently, that there was little difference in the country for endless miles in each direction. But there was a frown on his leathery face that did not go unnoticed by the lawman.

"Something bothering you?"

The army scout jerked a thumb toward their back trail. "Been a rider tailing us ever since about noon."

Rossiter twisted about, and shading his eyes with a cupped hand, threw his glance to the south. It took several moments in the late afternoon haze and shimmering heat, but eventually he located the party—a small dot in the far distance.

"Only some pilgrim, I reckon," he said, settling back into his saddle. "Maybe he'll keep coming and join us when we make camp."

"Maybe," Jubal said, shifting his cud from one cheek to the other, "but he sure don't seem anxious. He's been that close ever since I spotted him."

★ 11 ★

They had camped the night before in a shallow just off the road. Duke, glum after his pronouncement to the effect that he was of a mind to forget about the money he and Rube Brodie had hidden, said little during the evening and gave only monosyllabic replies when spoken to.

He was no different the following morning, even when it became necessary to hurriedly swing off into the mesquite and chaparral to avoid a quartet of riders coming from the direction of Pine Valley.

Nella, too, was mostly silent, but around noon a change came over her. With the horses traveling at an easy lope, she rode in close to Duke, and reaching out, laid a hand on Duke Finley's arm.

"I'm sorry," she said.

He frowned, turned to her. "Yeh? For what?"

"About what I said yesterday—about you and me. I guess I was all out of sorts, thinking about Rube and feeling a little sorry for myself. It's been a hard row to hoe, Duke—you've got to remember that and kind of make allowances."

Duke continued to frown as the meaning of her words gradually sank in. They were now passing through low, sandy hill country, with many bluffs and buttes in evidence. Here and there large rocks, bronze in the driving sunlight, thrust themselves up out of the reddish soil, and a solitary cedar, looking lonely and out of place among the hardier, more agressive yuccas and chollas, was a silhouette on the skyline.

"I ain't for certain what you're talking about."

"About us, Duke," Nella said, casting a side glance at Kissler, a stride or two behind them. Ferd was engrossed in contemplating the landscape to the west and south.

"You saying you've changed your mind—that you'll go to Mexico with me?"

The woman smiled, loosened the collar of her shirt. It had been cool, almost cold earlier that morning when they had roused and made coffee to go with the meat and bread purchased in Cougar Ridge. But now, with the sun climbing rapidly, the heat was beginning to be noticeable.

"That's just what I'm saying—"

Duke rocked back in his saddle, shouted for joy. Both horses, startled by the unexpected sound, shied briefly, and then recovering, resumed their steady pace. Ferd Kissler looked first at Duke and then to Nella, but his blank face revealed neither curiosity nor irritation at being excluded from whatever was happening.

"That sure is good news!" Duke said, almost beside himself with happiness. "I was feeling mighty down after what you said yesterday—lower'n a snake's belly—but right now I'm setting on the moon!"

"So am I," Nella said. "I don't know why I talked the way I did."

"I just couldn't savvy that, either," Finley said. "Me and a whole sackful of money—that'd be real hard for any gal to turn down." He paused, grinned. "I ain't saying I'm such a fine catch but, well, you and me, we've sort've been together a lot and we know each other good—so what'd be better than the pair of us

57

teaming up. We'd be rich, could settle down on a fine place in Mexico and enjoy life?"

"It all sounds wonderful, Duke," Nella said, looking ahead, "so wonderful I can hardly believe it. . . . Is that a road up there, coming in from the east?"

Duke, without raising his gaze, said, "Yeh, goes to Texas. Was probably where them four jaspers we met was coming from."

"Do we turn onto it to get to where you hid the money?"

"Nope, we keep going north. . . . Damn, it sure makes me feel good, you saying you'll tie up with me. Something I been wanting for years. In fact, I ain't—"

"Two riders following us," Ferd Kissler sang out suddenly. "Ain't for sure, but I think one of them's that sheriff."

Duke pulled up sharply, wheeled to face Kissler. Wordless, he reached for the telescope the gambler was holding and raised it to an eye.

"Pretty far," Ferd said. "Can't tell much about them—"

After a bit Finley lowered the glass and returned it to its owner. Nella, leaning forward on her saddle as she rested herself, studied Duke narrowly.

"Well, is it him?" she asked finally, her voice sharp.

"I reckon so," Duke replied, staring off into the east. "Can't swear to it but it sure looks like him."

"It'll be foolish to take any chances on it. Did you recognize the man with him?"

"Ain't for certain about that, either, but he looks like old Jubal Seibert. He was once a scout for the army. Lived with the Indians, but he's got hisself a shack there in Cherryville now."

"Why would the sheriff have him along," Nella began and broke off. "A tracker! That's why he brought him," she finished, answering her own question.

"Means something else for damn sure," Kissler said sourly, closing the telescope and returning it to his saddlebags. "We better find a good place and set up an ambush——"

"No," Duke said with a shake of his head. "We'd lose too much time. I got a better idea."

"You figured you had a better idea back there at the start," the gambler said coldly. "Didn't work. If you'd listened to me, let me put a bullet in that john law——"

"Forget it!" Duke snarled. "Hell, I wouldn't listen to you about nothing!"

"What can we do, then?" Nella asked, keeping her tone quiet, concerned. "They've gained on us—and they're getting closer all the time."

"That's because we ain't been hustling right along," Kissler commented dryly. "We ought've kept right at it, rode hard like they're doing. Now we're caught in a tight spot."

"No, reckon not," Finley drawled. "Seth's got old Jubal along to do the tracking in case he loses our trail. Now, that's real fine—we'll just give Jubal a little work. . . . Let's go."

Abruptly, Duke Finley wheeled about, and keeping to the center of the road where the prints of the horses' hoofs were clearly visible in the loose soil, he continued on.

They rode for a good hour, and then when they reached the turnoff that led east to Texas, he veered onto it—again making no effort to conceal their tracks.

"Why are we going this way?" Nella asked at once. "You said the money was——"

"Just you keep your shirt on," Duke replied. "I got a trick or two up my sleeve that'll get rid of Seth, and his friend, for certain this time."

A long two hours later they were well into the broken country and following an established road that cut its way along the floor of a valley paralleled by fairly high hills.

"This here's the road to Texas," Duke said, finally deciding to explain.

"You told me that," Nella remarked a bit tartly.

"Well, Seth Rossiter knows I sort of favor Texas, and I'm scheming to make him think that's where we're headed."

"You ain't going to fool him," Kissler said with a shrug. "And he's got himself a tracker who'll spot—"

"Just you keep your trap shut and wait and see," Duke broke in angrily. "I know what I'm doing!"

Near the middle of the afternoon, with the land gradually changing as they rode steadily east, toward the area commonly called the panhandle, they reached a small settlement placed in the center of an oasislike swale. There was nothing more to it than a general store and an accompanying saloon built near a spring, but it served its purpose as a break for those making the long, desolate journey from Texas to points farther west.

As they pulled up to the spring and dismounted, an elderly man, with an equally elderly woman at his side, came out of the weather-bleached building and paused in the shade of the porch.

"Howdy," the oldster greeted.

Duke and Ferd nodded and Nella smiled as the horses slaked their thirst. After a bit Finley turned about. "We on the right road to Texas?" he asked.

The old man bobbed. "Sure are—and it's a powerful long way to the next town. You best stock up on your needings while you're here—just like you're filling up with my water."

"Just what we aim to to," Duke said, and nodded to Nella Brodie. "You know what we're running short of. Why'n't you go inside, buy what we're needing. Me and Ferd'll look after the canteens while you're gone."

They spent a half hour at the place—Harper's Spring, the old man said it was called, although Duke could not recall it ever before having a name other than just the Spring.

Back in the saddle and ready to depart, he pointed

to the road leading east from the small circle of green grass, shading trees, water, and shabby structure.

"We keep following that to get to Texas?"

"Exactly what you do! First town'll be Mesa Flats. Take you maybe three days—"

"We're heading for Fort Worth—"

"Well, you'll find it a mighty long ride, but you just keep bearing east and you'll get there."

"Much obliged," Finley said, and nodding to the others, moved on.

★ 12 ★

"This don't make sense," Seth Rossiter said.

He was standing in the road with Jubal Seibert at his side, studying the three sets of tracks which indicated, without doubt, that Duke and his friends had turned off the main route and were heading east for Texas.

"Can't argue with them hoofprints," Jubal said, shrugging.

"I'm not—but why would Duke want to go to Texas? That money's hid out around here somewhere—there's no doubt of it."

Seibert helped himself to a corner from his plug of tobacco, shifted it about inside his mouth, and then relegated it to the hollow of a cheek.

"Was—maybe," he said. "You forgetting that him and them others spent some time in Cougar Ridge? He could've had the money hid out there—or maybe somewhere along the way twixt here and there. He's picked it up and's lighting out for Texas, where your badge ain't no good."

"He's wrong there," the lawman said grimly. "I'll follow him clean to hell if I have to. But you could be right," he added, staring off toward the hills, beyond which lay the panhandle country. "The money might've been in Cougar Ridge, but I can't see it that way. The bank he and Rube Brodie robbed was pretty far north of here—near Capital City. And Brodie got shot when they were leaving the place and died either the same day or the next, I don't remember which.

"Seems to me they would have cached the money up in that part of the country instead of bringing it way down here. Brodie wouldn't have been in any shape to do much riding."

"Maybe Duke moved it later on—"

"I don't think he had the chance. He got caught not long after."

"I'm beginning to smell a skunk," Jubal said, stroking his beard. "Them tracks are mighty plain. And something else—them four jaspers from over Texas way that was headed west, they said they didn't run into nobody coming down the road, when you asked them. Well, for sure, Duke and his friends were in between us and them."

"They hid out, didn't want to be seen," the lawman said, "and that means they for sure know we're trailing them."

"Yeh, and being real careful like—"

Rossiter nodded. Turning back to his horse, he swung up onto the saddle. "Well, nothing we can do but play the game with them. Let's move on."

"You aim to follow them up this road to Texas?" Jubal asked, climbing onto the buckskin.

"No choice—they took it. I know it's some kind of a trick, so we best keep a sharp eye on the tracks. They'll be cutting off somewhere."

Jubal threw his glance to the west as he gathered up the reins. "We got a few hours yet to dark. Can keep going till then."

"Probably all the time we'll need."

But the tracks continued far beyond the lawman's expectations, leading, finally, to a spring in a shaded hollow where there was a store and saloon being run by a man named Harper.

While the horses watered and Jubal refilled their canteens, Rossiter stepped up onto the porch, where the storekeeper leaned against a stanchion and eyed Jubal Seibert's activities sourly.

"Best you stock up on your trail grub here, same as you're doing with my water," he warned. "Ain't nothing 'tween here and the next town but a lot of dry ground and skinny varmints even the buzzards won't bother with."

"Obliged for the advice," Rossiter said. "We'll look our sack over, get what we need. There been anybody pass through here today? Would've been early."

"Well, yes, I reckon there was. They friends of your'n?"

"One of them—man called Duke—we used to punch cows together. I'm trying to catch up with him."

"You're on the right trail. Him and his woman and their friend are headed Texas way—Fort Worth. Was asking all about getting there."

"That the road they took?" Jubal asked, hanging the filled water containers back on the saddles.

"Sure is," the storekeeper said, pointing. "It's the only one out of here—unless you go back the way you come."

Jubal crossed to where the road left the shaded area of the spring and began to wind into the low, brushy hills. Halting, he dropped to his haunches, considered the ground briefly, and then doubled back to Rossiter.

"Them, all right. Three sets of tracks. Must've fixed that loose shoe. It don't show no more."

Harper drew up angrily. "What's the matter? Ain't you believing me when I tell you your friends headed east?"

Rossiter laughed, brushed the angry question aside with a wave of his hand. "My partner's an old army scout. Always has to have a look for himself. . . ."

We're obliged to you—"

"Ain't you figuring to buy something? It's a long ways to the first town—"

"Grub sack's in good shape—and we're traveling light," the lawman said, mounting his sorrel. Nodding to the storekeeper, and with Seibert close behind, he swung onto the road leading to Texas.

Almost immediately, he slowed, motioned the guide on ahead. "Still don't swallow this. Duke and me used to hang out around Fort Worth a lot, and him telling Harper he was going there sounds like it was for my benefit."

"And you're expecting them tracks to turn off somewheres—"

"That's it. If my hunch is right, they'll keep going east for a ways, and then at some place where it won't show up, Duke'll cut off and double back to Pine Valley."

Jubal nodded, moved on past the lawman, his eyes on the ground. "Sort of wishing we had us some field glasses. We could maybe see them up ahead, since they seen us."

"Like as not they've got glasses. My pair was in the saddlebags of the bay I was riding when they clubbed me. Could sure use them now, all right."

They continued in single file for the better part of a half mile, and then when the trail lifted up onto a broad, flinty mesa, the scout halted, dropped from his saddle, and began to examine the rock-studded soil more closely.

Walking slowly, he proceeded along the trail, confined at that point between bordering rows of chaparral and mesquite, halting now and then to look about or crouch and study the ground. Finally he faced the lawman.

"I ain't so certain about this, Sheriff," he said. "Been horses through here for sure. There's a-plenty of marks on the rocks and such—but maybe it ain't them. Maybe it was them four Texans we seen."

Rossiter gave that thought, raised his eyes, and looked east as far as the land contours would permit. The road, as near as he could determine, appeared hard-surfaced with partly buried rocks. If Duke and his party had turned off, he and Jubal could lose a lot of time continuing on to where they would find proof that such had taken place.

Twisting about, one hand resting on the saddlehorn, the other on the cantle, he gave the surrounding country quick scrutiny. A line of bluffs rising to a fairly high point lay off to their left a quarter mile or so.

"Forget the trail," he said, turning back to Jubal. "Let's climb to the top of that ridge. Ought to be able to see anybody traveling—east or west—from there."

Jubal spat, pulled himself stiffly back onto the buckskin. "That's right smart thinking! I reckon we can see half way to yonder and back from that peak—and if Duke and them've lit out for Fort Worth or have turned around and are going to that there Pine Ridge—we'll be able to spot which."

★ 13 ★

It was only a game trail they were following when, after a mile or so on the road to Texas, Duke had chosen to turn off and start doubling back in the direction of Pine Valley.

The path allowed them to travel at a fair amount of speed, and near dark, with Nella and Ferd both irritable from the extra hours of riding they felt had been unnecessary, they reached the settlement.

Being nothing more than a scattering of houses grouped around a small, one-street business section, Pine Valley's chief reasons for existence were the cattle drives that passed within a mile or so east and the occasional travelers moving from the upper part of the territory to the lower, or vice versa.

"That there's the hotel," Duke said to Nella, pointing out a low, single-story adobe structure near the center of town. "You get us room, while I take care of our horses. Damn shoe's coming loose on mine again."

He had ignored Ferd Kissler, as if the man were not present. As they continued on for the hitchrack fronting the hostelry—the Antlers, so called apparently from the large set of elk horns mounted over the door—Nella turned to Duke.

"I'm not sure I know what you mean—"

"Oh, I reckon you do," Duke replied brusquely. "You wanting me to spell it out real plain?"

Several persons along the street glanced to them as they passed, all wondering no doubt who the strangers might be and their reason for being there.

Nella had glanced at Ferd, frowned, and then brought her attention back to Finley. "I'm wondering—do you think it's safe to stop here? What if the sheriff didn't fall for your trick?"

"Ain't no danger of that," Duke said. "He's half way to the Texas border by now, I'll bet! He knows I got a real soft spot for Fort Worth, and it'll seem natural to him that I'm headed for there. Besides, I planted the word good with the old man, Harper. Time Seth finds out he's been euchered, we'll be long gone."

"Maybe," Ferd said indifferently. "That sheriff's a lot smarter'n you figure."

"The hell! I'm the one that knows him real good!" Duke said, brushing his hat to the back of his head. "Me and him lived and worked together for a-plenty of years."

"Probably the answer," Kissler said quietly. "You've been so close to him that you can't see him for what he is—smart and cagey."

Duke snorted, shook his head, and as they drew up to the Antlers' hitchrack, put his attention again on the woman.

"Don't you go worrying none about the sheriff," he said. "We ain't never going to see Seth Rossiter again. You just get us all fixed up for tonight."

Nella came off her saddle slowly, wearily. "I'm awful tired, Duke. I think it'd be better if I get a room for myself, alone, and another one for you and Ferd. We can all use a good night's sleep."

Finley's jaw hardened and a brightness filled his eyes. "There you go bucking me again! Damnit, can't you do nothing I want? I'm getting a belly full of your—"

Two men standing on the porch of the saloon adjacent to the hotel had turned, were listening. Nella removed her hat, allowed her trapped hair to loosen and fall down about her shoulders. "All right, Duke," she murmured. "Whatever you say."

"Now, that's my woman!" Finley said, his features brightening in expectation. "Won't need to take in your blanket roll—just your saddlebags and your extra duds."

Ferd Kissler had stepped down from the horse he was riding. Arm extended, he offered the reins to Duke so that, with Nella's mount, he could also be led to the livery stable.

"Hell with you!" Duke flared, refusing to accept the leather lines. "Take care of your own horse."

"It won't hurt you any to do it," Nella said in an exhausted voice. "You're going there, and Ferd can help me get—"

"You don't need no help getting a room—"

Kissler swore deeply, and pivoting, dropped back to his horse and swung up onto the saddle. His mouth a taut line, he wheeled about and rode off toward the livery stable. Duke watched him for a few moments and then, grinning, looked at Nella.

"Just what I'm hoping for—riling him up! Sure wish there was some way to get rid of him permanent. . . . Now, you go on in and fix us up with that room. I'll come along soon as I'm done at the livery stable."

"I'd like to clean up—take a bath—and we ought to eat."

"Sure, sure! You just tell the hotel man to send you up a tub and some hot water. I could do with a little washing up myself, so tell him to figure on a-plenty. Then when we're done scrubbing, we'll get a bite to eat."

Nella sighed, "All right, Duke," she said quietly, and turned away.

Finley cut his gray about immediately, and spurring the worn animal vigorously, hurried off at a fast trot. Reaching the low flat-roofed barn which stood at the opposite end of the street, Finely veered into the runway and dropped lightly to the ground.

"Got two horses here that's needing some looking after," he stated to the hostler, who came out of a tack room deeper in the shadowy structure. "First off, however, the gray's got a loose shoe. Tried fixing it myself down the trail a ways but it didn't hold. Want it done good this time—the blacksmith around?"

The hostler, a middle-aged man wearing a faded linsey-woolsey shirt, overalls, and thick-soled shoes, nodded. "Yeh—just hold on for a minute—"

Anxious to return to the hotel, and Nella, Duke shifted impatiently. "Hell, you can tell him what I'm wanting—"

The hostler made no reply as he disappeared into the tack room. Moments later he returned, a squat, thick-shouldered, black-bearded man with him.

"Best you tell Jacob so's he'll get it straight," the stableman said.

Finley immediately made known his requirements— a simple job of resetting the shoe and nailing it firmly in place. Jacob listened solemnly, stepped up to the gray, and rapping him gently on the leg, had his look at the problem.

"Sure," he said. "This I can fix for you right soon. Is it a hurry you are in?"

"Nope, don't aim to leave until morning."

Jacob's massive shoulders stirred. "He will be ready in thirty minutes, anyway. The charge is fifty cents, which I will have now."

Finley dug a coin out of a pocket, handed it to the smith, and as Jacob led the gray away, he turned to the hostler. "Want both my horses grained and watered. Will you see to it?"

"What I'm here for, ain't it?" the hostler said peevishly. "Sure, I'll take care of them."

Finley wheeled and hurried along the runway to the street. It occurred to him at that moment that he had not seen Ferd Kissler in the livery barn, and guessed the gambler had made arrangements for his horse and had gone on—probably to pass away the time in one of the saloons.

A drink would do him some good, too, Duke decided, walking quickly along the darkening street. Besides, he reckoned he ought to give Nella a little time to fix up and get ready, and such. The open doorway of a saloon appeared on his right, and not hesitating, he entered and bellied up to the bar.

The place was empty except for the owner and one patron at the counter. Finley called for a whiskey, downed it in a single gulp, signaled for a refill, and tossed it off. Paying, he pivoted on a heel and continued on to the hotel.

Stepping up to the desk, he nodded to the young clerk who greeted him with a forced smile.

"My wom . . . wife—she just came in here. What room's she in?"

"Three," the clerk said, frowning. "Right down the hall—to your left. You for sure that you—"

Duke Finley was already hurrying down the dark corridor, eyes searching eagerly for the designated room. He came to the door bearing a crudely painted 3 on its scarred surface. Grasping the knob, he turned it, threw the panel open—and came to a dead halt.

Nella and Ferd stood in the center of the room. Arms about each other, lips together, they were locked in a kiss.

At Finley's abrupt entrance Nella jerked back, a small cry escaping her throat as her hand went to her mouth in fear. Kissler wheeled, hand dropping to the pistol on his hip.

At that moment, a yell of anger and frustration and utter disappointment exploding from his gaping mouth, Duke lunged. One hand gripped Kissler's wrist, preventing him from drawing his weapon; the other, balled into a rock-hard fist, smashed into the man's jaw.

Nella cried out as Ferd went to his knees. She rushed forward, tried to place herself between the two men. Duke knocked her aside with a sweep of his arm and drove another blow into Kissler's jaw. Ferd groaned, went over backward, and sprawled loosely on the faded carpet.

Relentless, Finley bent over the man's limp figure. Reaching down, he grasped the front of the dazed Kissler's shirt front, jerked him upright, and drew back his arm for a third shocking blow.

"No, Duke—no!"

Nella Brodie's voice was like a knife cutting through the yellow haze that gripped Finley. He hesitated, anger pulsing through him like a hurried heartbeat. And then, in that moment of indecision, the woman threw herself at him, literally knocked him away from the helpless Ferd.

"You'll kill him!" Nella screamed.

Duke, heaving for wind, sweat clothing his body, let his arms fall to his sides as he drew himself upright. Eyes still burning, he faced the woman.

"I ought—I purely ought," he grated in a tight voice. "And you right along with him!"

Wheeling, he turned to the door, rigidly left the hotel, and getting his horse, rode north out of town.

★ 14 ★

"I sure can't see nothing of them," Jubal said as, slowly pivoting, he gazed out across the land.

It was, Seth Rossiter admitted, pretty much a waste of time and effort to climb to the ridge in hopes of seeing signs of Duke Finley and his friends. The nearby intervening hills shut off a view of the immediate surrounding area on all sides, and the flats beyond them were too distant to distinguish anyone on the move.

If he'd had his field glasses he might have a chance of spotting the outlaws—but he didn't and it was damn foolishness to do any wishing for them.

"Ought to be seeing some dust, seems," Jubal said, his squinting eyes now fixed on the country to the east. "Mighty hard to think their horses wouldn't stir up a little sign—even on hard ground."

"They could be out there somewhere, and stopped for the night," the lawman said, glancing at the lowering sun. "Going to be dark in a couple of hours."

"Yeh, I reckon they could be making camp," Seibert said, and came about to face Rossiter. "That what you want to do—set up here till it's night and see if we can locate their fire?"

Seth gave that consideration. "Would mean we'd be here for quite a spell, and if there wasn't any campfire, then we'd be out a lot of time—for nothing. I figure I don't have even one minute to waste if I'm to nail Duke before he picks up that money and gets away."

The scout nodded, began to chew thoughtfully on the bit of tobacco he'd just gnawed from his plug.

"Can sure bet he'll take off like a turpentined cat quick as he lays his hands on it. And a man sure could get hisself lost good with thirty thousand dollars to sort of smooth the way!"

"Expect Brodie's widow, Nella, and that fellow she's with, Kissler, will be claiming a chunk of it—maybe half."

"You know Duke pretty good. You figure he'll divvy up without a fuss?"

"Not sure. Duke was always pretty easygoing and got along with about everybody. Did always like to have his own way, however, so I'm not certain how he'll act when it comes to something like this. He just might take it in his head to hang on to all of that money."

"Unless he hatches up a bargain of some kind with the woman."

"Bargain?"

"Well, I heard you say she was a good looker, and Duke ain't very old. He might just talk her into throwing in with him, and then both of them taking off with the cash."

"Could be how he's got it doped out. Duke always did have a hankering for the ladies. . . . Expect we best be climbing down off here and moving on."

"Yep, reckon so. What are you aiming to do next—head for Texas or go on back toward Pine Valley?"

The lawman, slipping and sliding on the loose gravel as he descended the bluff, made no reply until both had reached the foot of the grade and were walking to where their horses waited.

"Was thinking it'd be easy to tell if they doubled back to the road for Pine Valley. They'd cross somewhere above us if they did. That make sense to you?"

"Yeh, reckon it does. If we find tracks, we'll know for damn sure they ain't going to Texas—but if we don't, then we're going to wind up out of luck for certain."

Rossiter nodded. "It's a chance I'm willing to take, Jubal. I just don't think Duke's going to Fort Worth." Glancing over a shoulder, he assessed the sun. "We've got a while yet till dark. What do you say we look for signs of them crossing back?"

Seibert made no comment, simply swung up onto his horse, and pointed the little buckskin north.

"Expect you're thinking straight," he said as the lawman rode up alongside him. "And spotting them tracks won't be no chore. This here dirt ain't like that over there, full of rocks and such. This is sort of soft and loose and the marks'll show up real plain."

Rossiter leaned forward, studied the red-brown soil. It looked firm to him and he failed to distinguish even the hoof prints that the old guide's buckskin was leaving, but then he wasn't much of a tracker, he had to admit.

They pressed on as the sun dropped lower and the shadows began to lengthen. Jubal, now out in the lead, was proceeding slowly and occasionally halted entirely while he left the saddle to examine more closely an imprint on the ground. At such times Seth Rossiter restrained his impatience with difficulty, aware that with each passing moment Duke Finley could be getting farther beyond his reach, but knowing also that such delays were necessary if he were to again get on the outlaw's trail.

If Duke was making for Fort Worth, it could only mean that he had recovered the money he and Rube Brodie had stolen in the bank robbery and later hidden. But if true, where could the hiding place have been? It was logical to think that if he picked up the money at Cougar Ridge, and had in mind to go to Texas, he would have ridden east out of that settlement and not continued north.

Evidently—still assuming that he now had the thirty thousand dollars—the cache had been somewhere along the road between that settlement and where it turned off to go east. That could mean anywhere, as there were no towns, no stores, not even a homesteader's shack or an abandoned ranchhouse along the route until Harper's Springs was reached. Rossiter doubted very much if the outlaws had stashed the stolen money near Harper's place; the risk that the crusty old storekeeper might discover and keep it was too great.

Also, Rossiter did not believe that Duke and Rube, or Duke alone, was in the area after the bank holdup. No, if the outlaw had retrieved the money, it would have been somewhere back on the main road connecting Cougar Ridge with Pine Valley.

And if Duke now had the money and was riding to Fort Worth—what should he do? Follow, which he felt obligated to do since he had been the one the outlaw escaped from, or should he return to Cherryville and turn the matter over to Deputy U.S. Marshal J. W. Hill, who had the authority to enter Texas in pursuit of a criminal?

The hell with that! Rossiter angrily discarded the thought. He'd not permit his lack of authority to cross the state's border keep him from tracking down Duke Finley! He was not about to let his one-time saddle partner cheat the law or put a black mark on his record as a lawman! He'd chase—

"Here ya' are," Jubal Seibert's voice broke into Rossiter's deep reflections. "Reckon it's just how you figured."

The lawman was a few paces behind Seibert, had let his sorrel stay back while still keeping pace with the buckskin. Now, spurring forward quickly, he dismounted and crouched beside the squatting scout.

"You find the tracks?"

"Right there," the older man said, pointing to several faint indentations in the soil on what appeared to be a narrow path. "They're following a game trail—going west toward the main road. Ain't no doubt it's them. That shoe's coming loose on one of the horses again."

Rossiter's mouth tightened with satisfaction as he stood up and stared off across the flats. It was too late to continue. Darkness was almost upon them, but he knew definitely now which direction Duke and the others had taken, and it was not for Texas!

"We'll make camp here," he said, coming back to Jubal, who was standing by and waiting for Rossiter to give the word as to what was to be done next. "Can get an early start in the morning."

★ 15 ★

As Duke Finley strode angrily out of the stuffy hotel room and disappeared into the hallway, Nella hurried to Ferd Kissler and knelt beside him. There was alarm in her eyes but it was not solicitude for any possible injury the gambler had sustained from Finley's knotted fists, but concern that he might no longer be of any use to her.

"Are you bad hurt?" she asked, helping him to a sitting position.

Kissler, still somewhat dazed, gently rubbed his jaw and shook his head slowly. "Hell, no," he rasped, and then as his senses returned, struggled free of her and to his feet. Glancing about, he said, "Where is he? I'll kill that sonofabitch! I'll—"

"You'll back off, that's what you'll do," the woman said, restraining him. "You're not killing anybody, specially him!"

"The hell I'm not! I ain't letting no saddletramp knock me around—"

Nella looked away, smiled faintly. "Seems he did, at that," she murmured.

Kissler whirled on her. "You think it's a big laugh, eh? By God, I'll show you—him—"

Nella sobered, and reaching up, patted his whiskery cheeks dispassionately. "You forget it, Ferd—for a time, anyway," she said. "You'd be like that fool in the storybook who killed the goose that laid the golden eggs. We need Duke until he leads us to that money. Once he's done that—he's all yours."

Kissler's keyed-up manner eased slowly, reluctantly. "Yeh, you're right," he said, shrugging, and crossing to the washstand, filled the tin bowl with water from the china pitcher. Ducking his face, he soaked his head thoroughly, and then taking up the towel Nella handed to him, began to dry himself.

"I should've locked that damn door," he said, his voice thick from a crushed and swelling lip. "I knew he'd be coming. I was a fool to forget—"

"Like as not it all would have ended the same. He would have found you in here with me when we opened it. Mistake you made was coming in here in the first place."

The gambler nodded, said, "Guess you're right, but this fight's been brewing ever since we joined up—and it ain't finished yet, not by a damn sight! Next time he won't catch me looking the other way!"

"I know," Nella said gently, breaking in, "but that'll be later. Right now we've got to figure how to patch things up with him."

"That's going to be up to you—"

"Not entirely. One thing for sure, you're going to have some making up with him to do—tell him you lost your head, or something like that, and that you're sorry."

Ferd, a frown on his forehead, tossed the towel aside, and walking to the window, glanced out. It was growing dark. As he watched the few persons visible on the street going about their business, he heard Nella scrape a match into flame and light the lamp that sat on the table.

"Ain't for sure I can do that," he said. "Be the same as eating dirt, and I ain't no hand to—"

"Not even for thirty thousand dollars?"

Kissler came about. His mouth now looked twice its normal size. His lips had continued to swell, and a dark area had appeared on the left side of his face, mute evidence of the power in Duke Finley's fists. After a few moments' consideration of Nella's words, his shoulders lifted, fell in resignation.

"For that much money—and you—I reckon I could do most anything," he said, facing her squarely. "But you're going to have to do some fast talking, too. It wasn't only me standing there. You was doing your part."

Nella smiled, sat down on the edge of the bed. The corn-shuck mattress rustled noisily as it accepted her slight weight.

"I enjoyed it," she said, and then waved him back as he impulsively started toward her. "We've got some thinking to do, Ferd, and we've got to be careful from now on. We can't let something like this happen again—Duke's already threatened to just forget about the money, leave it where it's hid."

"When was this?"

"When I sort of slipped up and told him I'd not go to Mexico with him, that I had my own plans. I had to straighten that out in a hurry."

Kissler raised a hand, explored his jaw tenderly as he gave that thought. Then, "You figure he'd for sure ride off and leave thirty thousand dollars buried somewheres, or was he trying to scare you?"

Nella rose, wet a part of the towel from the water in the bowl, and returning to her place on the bed, began to dab at her face.

"Yes, he would. He's nothing but a big, dumb cowboy who's never had anything more'n the clothes on his back and maybe a dollar or two in his pockets, and he's stupid enough to do something like that if he gets worked up enough about it. How and why Rube ever teamed up with him, I'll never puzzle out."

"Way he talks, they were partners for a long time and he always had his eye on you—"

"That's his story, and maybe it's true. But I hardly noticed him. . . . Where do you suppose he went?"

Ferd turned again to the window. It was entirely dark outside now and he could see the glow of lamp-light coming from a store window.

"Expect we'll find him in a saloon."

"Probably. Go see if you can find him . . . no, we both had better go. If you're by yourself, the two of you will start fighting again. I'll be ready in a minute."

Nella felt the eyes of the hotel clerk, standing behind his makeshift counter, upon her and Ferd as they came out of the hallway into the small, empty lobby. Boldly, she ignored his curiosity and nodded. "Looking for that friend of ours—the man who came here a bit ago and then left, probably in a hurry."

"Said he was your husband—"

"My husband? You must've heard wrong."

"What he claimed," the clerk declared stubbornly. "Anyways, that ruckus I heard—you'll have to pay for whatever you busted up—chairs and such."

"Nothing got busted," Nella said. "You know where he went?"

"Nope. Walked straight through here like he was ready to eat horseshoes, and headed down the street."

"Which way?"

"Toward the livery stable."

Nella threw a hasty, worried glance to Ferd, and then together they continued across the lobby and entered the street. Halting abruptly, Kissler laid a hand on the woman's arm.

"Maybe he ain't gone. Let me have a look in the saloon before we go any farther."

He was back in only moments. "He's not in there.

Could be in that one a bit on down. Can stop by there on the way to the stable."

Nella's lips were set. "I've got a feeling he's gone."

"Maybe. We'll know for sure when we get to the stables."

Duke was not in either of the two saloons that lay en route, and Nella's conviction proved to be true when they roused the hostler at the livery barn and made their inquiry.

"Rode out of here thirty, forty minutes ago," the man said. "Come in, saddled up his horse hisself, paid me, and left."

"Headed north?"

The hostler nodded, jerked a thumb in that direction. "That's the way he went—north, toward Bitter Creek."

"It very far?" Nella asked.

"Day and a half, ordinary riding."

"That means he'll be making camp for the night, probably not far from here," she said to Kissler as they walked slowly back to the wide doorway.

Reaching the entrance to the barn, she stepped out into the street, filled now with night's cool softness and the muted sounds of families at ease after the day's work. Glancing back to be certain she was beyond ear-shot of the hostler, Nella turned to Ferd.

"We'll have to go after him. You get the horses ready while I go back to the hotel for my stuff. He hasn't had time to eat, so I'll drop by the general store and pick up some of the things he likes. When we find him, I'll' cook him up a meal—that'll make him feel better."

"I don't reckon he's gone far," Kissler said. "It's been a hard day and that horse of his is plenty beat."

"Want you to go back to one of the saloons, get a quart of whiskey," Nella went on, ignoring Ferd's observation as if not hearing. "And while I'm thinking about it, when we find him I don't want you get all riled up over what I'll have to do to patch things up. Just you remember it'll all be because of the money—not because he means one damn whit to me. Understand?"

Ferd's shoulders stirred. "Sure, I savvy. I ain't liking it one bit, but as I said, for thirty thousand dollars I can do about anything I need to."

Nella smiled, turned away. "Just keep on thinking that," she said, and hurried off into the night.

★ 16 ★

"You see any more of that pilgrim you figured maybe was trailing us?" Seth Rossiter said as they topped out a rise and looked down upon the settlement of Pine Valley.

"Was wondering when you'd be asking," Jubal replied testily. It had been a long, hot day, and weariness showed in his lined face and watery eyes. "He's still back there—just keeping pace with us."

The lawman leaned forward on his saddle, eased the muscles of his back and legs. "He follow us when we cut off onto the road to Texas?"

Seibert spat tobacco juice, wagged his head. "Wouldn't know that—was a mite busy about then. Maybe he did and maybe he didn't, but he's sure there now, dogging our tracks."

Rossiter shrugged, wiped all thought of the pilgrim, whoever he was, from his mind; he had other things to think about, and the lone rider no doubt was just a traveler taking his time en route to somewhere.

He'd not find Duke and his two friends in Pine Valley, the lawman was certain. His luck hadn't been running that good, but there was the possibility Finley had laid over for a length of time and thereby narrowed the gap between them.

"We staying here the night?" Jubal asked as they turned into the main street and angled for the hitchrack in front of the squat Antlers Hotel.

"Don't know yet," Rossiter replied. "Depends on how long ago since Duke and the others rode out."

"Well, we ain't getting much more out of these here horses—or me either, if you're wanting my opinion."

Rossiter pointed to the saloon adjacent to the hotel. "Go on in there and get yourself a couple of drinks while I do some asking around. Maybe it'll make you feel better."

"I'm feeling fine. It's these here horses I'm fretting over," the old scout said, drawing to a halt and sliding to the ground.

Standing there in the strong sunlight, ignoring the glances of a half a dozen or so persons nearby who were eyeing him—bearded, fringed doeskin shirt, baggy pants, and moccasins—he let his glance rest on the saloon's entrance.

"Reckon a snort wouldn't hurt none. Where'll I meet you?"

"Livery stable—on down a ways," the lawman said, pointing. "Can leave the horses there if we decide to stay over."

Jubal grunted, and tying the buckskin to the rack's crossbar, wheeled and padded quietly up to the doorway of the saloon and disappeared into it.

Rossiter kneed his horse on up to the rack and swung down. After securing the sorrel, he crossed the hotel's porch and stepped inside. The lobby, small and shadowy, was deserted, but there was a man standing behind a counter affair that served as a desk who greeted him with an expectant smile.

"You needing a room, friend?"

"Maybe later," the lawman said. "Right now I'm

looking for some information. Three people—two men and a woman—"

"Was here last night—or I reckon I ought to say part of the night," the clerk broke in.

"What's that mean?"

"Them two fellows got in a scrap—right down there in Room Three—over the lady, I guess it was, then the big one lit out."

Trouble between Duke and Ferd Kissler. Evidently matters were not going very well, the lawman thought. That could work to his advantage.

"What about the woman and the other man?" he asked.

"Took off, too, but it was a while after. Then she come back and got her belongings, paid me for the whole night, and left again. Heard later that they rode out of town."

"What time was all this?"

"Was getting on to midnight, as I recollect."

Rossiter swore quietly. The outlaws still had a long lead on him. Putting his attention again on the clerk, he said, "You know if they all left town—all three of them?"

"Can't answer that, mister. Best way to find out if you're needing to know is go talk to Abe Salmon at the livery stable. And you might go see Pete Ferguson—he owns the general store, and somebody said the woman was in there buying up a lot of fancy grub just before they pulled out."

Rossiter nodded. "Obliged to you," he said. "I'll talk to Salmon. He'll be the one who can tell me what I want to know."

"What about a room?" the hotel man said hurriedly.

The lawman gave the matter thought. With Duke that far ahead of him there was little sense in pushing on. If it had been only hours, it would be different; he would consider renting fresh horses and continuing—but that was not the case. It would be better to give their own mounts a good night's rest and feed, and then ride hard that coming day.

"Be needing one, for my partner and me," he said, thinking that Jubal should be pleased and that his griping would now cease—at least for a while. "Can look for us back in about an hour. There a good place to eat around here?"

"Next door," the hotelman said, and smiled. "Ain't just good—it's the only place."

Rossiter grinned. "I reckon it'll have to do, then," he said, and returned to the street.

He wasn't particularly fond of walking, which was true, more or less, of all men accustomed to riding, but it felt good to have solid ground under his feet. Instead of going onto the saddle, he grasped the sorrel's lines in his left hand and led the animal along the dusty roadway to the livery barn.

"You Abe Salmon?" he asked of the overall-clad man who came forward at once from a stall at the end of the runway.

"What I been told. What can I do for you?"

"Take care of my horse, for one thing—and my partner's. He'll be along in a bit. Man at the hotel said you could give me some information on three people who were here last night."

Salmon scratched at the side of his head. "Only folks around here last night, besides a couple that lives here, was a woman and two men."

"They're the ones I mean."

"Men'd been fighting. One of them come got his horse not much after he'd left it here. He was looking all right—sort of riled up, but all right. Other'n looked like he'd walked into a threshing machine."

"Man at the hotel said there'd been an argument—"

"Argument, hell! It must've been a stemwinder of a knock-down and drag-out!"

"Sounds like it. The big man—one you say wasn't in

too bad a shape—did I understand that he got his horse and rode off ahead of the others?"

"Yep, that's what he did. Had Jacob—he's the blacksmith—fix a loose shoe on the gray he was riding. Old Jacob hadn't been done working on the gray more'n a half hour when the fellow showed up, wanting him."

For the second time Jubal wouldn't have the gray's defective hoofprint to serve as a guide. "He head north?"

"That's what he done. Must've been figuring to make camp somewheres along the road. Takes a day and a half at best to get to Bitter Creek, the next town."

"Did the woman and the other man follow him?"

"Yeh, that's it. Seemed real anxious to catch up with him, too. They friends of yours?"

"More or less," Rossiter said, and turned as the sound of a horse approaching reached him. "Expect that'll be my partner."

Jubal, astride the buckskin plodding softly through the ankle-deep dust of the street, veered into the stable's runway and halted alongside Rossiter's sorrel.

"We staying?" he asked, his tone almost belligerent.

The lawman nodded. "We are. Salmon here'll take care of the horses. We've got us a room at the hotel and there's a place to get supper next door."

"Good," Seibert said, sliding off his saddle. "Eating's been mighty lean on this sashay, seems to me. I can use a fair-sized, stove-cooked meal."

"You're about to get it," Rossiter said, and bobbing to the stableman, wheeled and started back up the street with Jubal Seibert at his shoulder.

★ 17 ★

Duke Finley was hunched beside his low fire when he heard horses coming. Trailwise, he immediately rose and faded back into the brush beyond the flare of yellow light, and hand resting on the butt of his pistol, waited. Moments later he saw that it was Nella and Ferd Kissler.

They halted at the edge of camp, and Nella, dropping hurriedly from her saddle, called out, "Duke?"

Her voice was strained, anxious, and seeing her standing there, turned golden by the fire's glow, Duke felt the old persistent longing stir through him once again. Maybe he had acted too quickly, maybe there was an explanation to what he had seen. Nella did appear worried—like she was scared she'd lost him. Well, he'd just teach her a lesson, straighten her out a bit on how she'd better handle herself around other men if she was going to be his woman!

"Duke?" she called again.

"I'm here," he answered quietly, and stepped out of the shadows.

A small cry escaped Nella's lips. Rushing to him, she threw her arms about his neck. Finley barely

89

stirred, but stood rigid, hands loose at his sides, enjoying his moment of victory.

"I . . . I was so worried when I found you had gone on without me," Nella cried, pulling back to look up at him. "I wanted to explain—"

"That bastard's still along," Duke cut in harshly, ducking his head at Kissler. "You want to explain that?"

"I can't help it, Duke! I owe him for helping me, and he says he's going to stick with us until he gets paid."

"I can pay him off right now—with a bullet," Finley said in a low, savage voice.

"No—that would be a mistake! We . . . you can put up with him until we get the money, can't you? And that won't be much longer, will it? We must be close to where you and Rube hid it."

Duke made no reply to the leading question, just continued to stare at Ferd Kissler, still on his horse and listening in silence to what was being said. After a time he bucked his head at the gambler.

"I reckon he can step down, but, by God, he sure better stay plenty clear of you! I even see him with his hands on you again, I'll kill him so quick he'll think he was lightning-struck!"

"He won't ever touch me again—not ever—"

"That's sure how it better be. I still don't savvy what he was doing in our room—holding and kissing you like he was."

Nella sighed deeply, shook her head. "It has always been like that for me, Duke," she said sadly. "Men are always wanting to kiss me. I don't know what it is about me that makes some of them act like they do, but it's a big problem. They just seem to want to grab me, take me in their arms.

"It used to make Rube furious until he finally understood. You've got to believe that times like that—like there in that hotel tonight—aren't really my fault. And the men that do it don't mean a thing to me—or me to them. It's sort of a notion, an impulse, on their part."

Nella paused, studied Duke's set features carefully. Beyond her Ferd Kissler had dismounted, was standing beside his horse. Back on the flats a coyote barked into the night, and off in the direction of Pine Valley two quick gunshots echoed hollowly through the hush.

"Well, that's one damn thing I sure aim to change now that me and you're teaming up," Duke said firmly.

"I hope so," Nella agreed. "You're the kind who'll look after a wife, and other men will see that and not be taking advantage of her. They'll be afraid—"

"They sure better be!" Duke snapped. "I ain't letting nobody trifle around with my woman! You hear that, Kissler?"

Ferd nodded, said blandly, "Sure. Heard you the first time, too."

"Well, mister, this here's the last time I'm warning you, so you sure better watch your step—and you best keep clear of me, anyway. I just might change my mind sudden like and pay you off the way I want."

Kissler muttered something under his breath, and wheeling, began to unload his horse. Duke glared at the gambler's back for a long instant while anger stiffened him and filled his eyes with a glitter.

"Damn you! I reckon I'll—" he began, and then broke off as Nella stepped in front of him, and placing both hands on his chest, restrained him gently.

"Never you mind," she said placatingly, "let's us forget about him. I've brought you some things for supper. I knew you didn't take time to eat. Now, you just sit there by the fire and I'll fix a meal for you."

Duke's shoulders came down as he slowly relaxed. "Ain't had no supper, that's for sure. What'd you bring?"

"A home-baked pie—dried apricot—for one thing. And there's canned peaches, fresh bread and butter, some sliced beef roast, and coffee—real coffee, Arbuckles. And then for later on—"

Duke had backed up to the rock Nella had indicated and sat down. Throwing a handful of wood into the flames, he looked at her hopefully.

"What's for later?"

"I brought a quart of whiskey so's we could do some drinking together."

"Drinking," Finley repeated in a falling voice. "Hell, setting around drinking ain't nothing special."

"Maybe not, but what comes after that sure can be," the woman said coyly, and turning, retraced her steps to her horse.

Taking off her saddlebags and the flour sack of groceries purchased from the store in Pine Valley, she also removed her blanket roll. Tucking it under an arm she glanced to Ferd.

"You finish pulling off my gear, and then stake my horse out with the others," she said curtly, and started back to where Duke waited. She hesitated, again faced Kissler.

"Something else, I'd as soon you'd throw your blanket away from our fire. Might be better if you'd go ahead and make your own camp."

Ferd, in the act of unsaddling her mount, stopped. He seemed to think over her words for a bit, and then, resigned, resumed his chore while Nella continued toward the fire and Finley.

Sitting down beside him, she opened the flour sack and began to remove its contents. The pie was crushed, looked more like a fruit roll, and smilingly considering it, she placed it in his hands.

"This is all yours. I'm sorry it's in such a mess."

"Won't hurt the tasting none," Duke said, and started wolfing it down.

"You finish that," Nella said, now obtaining the small pot they had been using along the trail for coffee from her saddlebags. Getting to her feet, she added, "I'll get some water from my canteen."

Duke, mouth filled and swallowing noisily, watched her return to her saddle, slung over a clump of rabbit-bush by Kissler, and unhook her container of water. She paused briefly to have a few additional words with the gambler, and then, smiling, once more returned to Duke.

Kneeling, she filled the pot from the canteen and set it in the fire to heat. Finley, the pie almost gone, reached out, wrapped his fingers about her wrist and pulled her about. "I seen you talking to that bastard," he said accusingly. "What was you saying to him?"

Nella frowned, freed herself of his grip. "I just told him I was fixing something to eat and it would be ready pretty soon. We never got a chance to eat, either, Duke, being so upset about you—"

"The sonofabitch can starve, far as I give a damn!"

"I know, but we can't let him go hungry—no more'n we'd let a dog starve. It wouldn't be decent—not when we'll have plenty."

Finley stirred irritably. "Sure wishing you hadn't brung him along in the first place."

"I didn't have a choice," Nella explained in a patient voice, opening the sack of already ground coffee beans and dumping a generous handful into the now simmering pot. "I've told you that—and I guess we can't blame him for insisting on coming along to be sure he gets paid. It's only natural for him to not trust us, for after all, we're strangers to him. If you were in his boots, you'd look at it the same way he does."

"I reckon, but there's one thing I sure wouldn't do—I wouldn't fiddle around with another man's woman like he done. You never told me yet what he was doing in our room."

"I didn't? Forgot, I guess. He was there waiting for you—the same as I was—so we could go eat."

"He have hisself another room?"

93

"I suppose. I wasn't interested enough in him to ask," Nella replied, beginning to lay out the rest of the food on the flour sack, now serving as a tablecloth.

Duke watched her for a time, and then, "Heard you telling him to do his sleeping somewheres else. That mean that we—"

Nella turned, faced him direct. "Means just what it sounds like. We'll be putting our blankets together. I'm tired of sleeping alone."

Duke Finley rocked back in surprise and happiness. "Hallelujah!" he breathed huskily. "I been waiting for this night—for years!"

★ 18 ★

"You're going to run these here horses into the ground if you don't hold up a bit!" Jubal Seibert shouted above the drumming of hoofs.

Rossiter had set a fast pace when they left Pine Valley, well before first light. Glancing across to the army scout, he shook his head.

"They've had a night's rest and plenty of feed. Both in fine shape, and I aim to push them hard," he called back. "Duke and the others can't be more'n a day ahead of us now—maybe less—and I figure to have that trimmed by half, come sundown."

"Yeh, and you'll have a couple of wind-broke horses," Seibert predicted sourly.

The lawman only shrugged. Earlier he had begun to turn a deaf ear to the scout's continual protests concerning his overworking their mounts, relying entirely on his own judgment as to what the sorrel and the tough little buckskin could take. It had become obvious that it was Jubal who needed the rest, but the proud old man was simply refusing to admit that age was at last having its way with him and, consciously or not, was endeavoring to escape that fact.

Again Rossiter glanced at Seibert. He hadn't really

looked at the man before but he could see now that Jubal had grown old. He was expecting too much of him, he supposed, but up until that moment he had just taken things for granted, had assumed Seibert to be as he'd always known him—strong as a mule, untiring, able to withstand whatever came his way. It was odd how change could take place right before a man's eyes and he'd never see it, the lawman thought.

He'd have to look elsewhere for a man to do his tracking, Rossiter guessed—one younger, who could stand the hardships of the trail. But he'd have to do it carefully, bring it about in a way that it would not offend Jubal. He'd not do anything to break the old man's heart.

Of course that depended on whether he would still be a lawman when this was over, and he'd have need of a tracker. If Duke and his two friends recovered the money and got away from him, then he would be looking at an entirely different situation.

Certainly, other lawmen had lost prisoners and it had not brought an end to their careers. But this was different; they weren't him—Seth Rossiter—and the prisoner they lost likely hadn't been, at one time, their best friend. There was but one solution—he could not allow Duke Finley to get away.

Near noon a wind came up to whip at them from the east—from that blasted panhandle, Jubal had put it—and, heavy with sand and powder-fine dust, it slowed them some. But by nightfall, when they halted to make a dry camp, Seth still felt they had done well and had covered a considerable amount of ground.

He stood for a moment watching Seibert dismount, noting the man's slow, stiff movements with sadness, and then looking away so as not to let the older man become aware of his attention, he began to unsaddle his sorrel.

"If you'll get us a fire started and put some water on

for coffee, I'll look after the horses," Rossiter said over a shoulder.

Jubal nodded, offering no protest, and taking the grub sack containing the necessary articles from his saddle, carried them to the center of the swale where they had halted. Setting the sack aside, he began to collect wood for the fire.

Later, as they rested near the wavering flames, Rossiter sitting on his blanket, Seibert sprawled full length on his, drinking coffee, the lawman glanced upward to the now overcast sky.

"Could get rain, cool things off a mite. If it does, we can move a bit faster, maybe cut a few more miles off the lead Duke's got on us."

"A mile's a mile, and there ain't no making it no shorter," Jubal observed dryly.

"For sure, but a man can maybe cover it faster than somebody else if he keeps at it—and that's what I'm trying to do."

"And kill the horses—"

Rossiter stirred, looked off into the windy night. He was in no mood to argue with Seibert.

"I'm keeping a close eye on them. I'm not about to set us afoot."

"Well, you sure seem to be trying powerful hard. Come tomorrow, it'll be me saying how fast and how far my buckskin's going to go. I expect I know him a lot better'n you do."

"I reckon you do," the lawman said agreeably, but he had come to a decision. He could expect nothing but out and out interference from Jubal Seibert from there on—and that was one thing he could not have. Every minute given to the scout's complaining and holding back was time lost in overtaking the outlaws—time in which Duke and his partners would get even farther ahead. He had no choice now but to do something about it. When they reached Bitter Creek, the next town, he'd try to come up with an idea that would allow his old friend to pull out gracefully.

The answer came of its own accord the following morning. Rossiter had gotten them off to another early start despite Jubal's grumbling, but the lawman again closed his ears to objections; he had a feeling that he was drawing near to the outlaws and was permitting nothing to slow him down.

Around noon, as they topped out a high rise in the cedar-studded hill country through which they were passing, Jubal called a halt. "Horse of mine ain't acting right," he said as the lawman drew up beside him. "Best I breathe him for a spell."

Rossiter nodded. They had crossed the last few miles at a fast lope and even the sorrel had worked up a lather from his efforts. But it had been well worth it, Seth was certain; Bitter Creek would not be too far ahead now, and maybe—just maybe—Duke Finley would still be there.

"Yonder's that dang pilgrim," Jubal said, staring off to the south. "Ain't much more'n a speck, but there he is."

"Could be a different rider," Rossiter said, glancing to the sky. It had cleared to a scattering of clouds, and while no rain had come, it was some cooler.

"Nope, same one. Dark-colored horse," Seibert declared firmly. "Beats me how he just stays put—never gets no closer or farther back. I reckon he makes camp when we do, then moves out same time that we do."

"Sets a man to wondering, all right," Rossiter said. "Wish we had the time to wait for him somewhere, or double back and meet up with him. Could see then what it's all about—figuring he's nothing more'n a man going somewhere and taking it easy."

"You're wrong there, Sheriff," Jubal said. "That fellow ain't taking it easy! He keeps right up with us when we're riding like the heel flies was after us, and

98

then slows down when we do. There's some real important reason for him to be acting like he is."

"Just could be that you're right," the lawman said, "and I'd sure like to find out what's going on, but we don't have the time. . . . You ready to move out?"

Jubal spat, brushed at his mouth, and eyed his horse critically. "I reckon he is," he said, making it clear it was the buckskin that was under consideration.

They pressed on, Rossiter again setting a steady, fast pace that ended again, abruptly, when Seibert raised a hand, and catching the lawman's eye, wagged his head.

"Horse's gone lame," he said as they drew to a stop. "I knew it all along—he can't keep going on like we've been doing."

Rossiter looked off to the north. "I'm not sure how far we are from Bitter Creek. Half a day, I expect."

"Best thing's for you to go on," Jubal said. "Ain't no sense in me holding you back—and I know you're in an all-fired hurry to get to that town."

"Am, for a fact. Good chance Duke and his bunch'll be there—or nearby."

"Then smart thing's for you to keep moving. Me and the buckskin'll get there best we can—and don't do no waiting for me. If you've got to keep going—just you go right ahead. I'll get me another horse and catch up soon's I can."

"Seems the thing to do," Rossiter said. "Can you manage to get to that town all right?"

"Hell, yes! This ain't the first time a horse ever give out on me somewhere in the sticks. I'll make it, for certain—don't fret none about it."

"Good enough," Rossiter said with a smile, "I'll be looking for you later," and raking the sorrel with his spurs, hurried off down the road.

★ 19 ★

They were slow getting started that next morning, due, Duke said with a sly grin at Nella Brodie, to too much whiskey and too much woman. Throughout the night Kissler had maintained a distant position from the camp, as he'd been instructed to do, and did not put in an appearance until breakfast, when the woman summoned him.

The quick, thin meal of warmed bread, meat, and black coffee was eaten in silence, with only Duke displaying any enthusiasm, and the sun was well above the horizon to the east before they were finally mounted and on their way.

For the first three hours or so, with the horses holding to a steady lope, little was said, but as the day wore on Duke grew expansive and gradually crowding Nella's horse to one side until they were beyond Ferd Kissler's hearing, he began to talk of the times before Rube Brodie died from a lawman's bullet, and how great a future now lay ahead for the two of them.

"Rube would've wanted us to tie up together," he said. "Knowing him, he'd figure if he couldn't have you, he'd want me to."

"I doubt if he ever told you that," Nella said a bit

100

wearily. The night had been a hectic one and it was reflected by the haggard lines in her face.

"Well, maybe not right out, but that's sure how he'd want it—and him being my best friend—the best one I ever had, I reckon, save Seth Rossiter—I aim to see it works out that way. Sure am lucky you feel the same way."

Nella smiled, shifted wearily on her saddle and brushed at her heavy-lidded eyes. "Do we have to go much farther?"

Duke Finley grinned broadly. "You're real anxious to get started for Mexico, ain't you? Well, it won't be long now."

"How long?" Nella pressed.

"Just a few more days—four, maybe five."

"Till we get to where you hid the money?"

"Yeh, we're going the wrong way for Mexico. Soon as I get my hands on the cash, we'll head straight back—only this time we'd maybe better swing over through Texas. I ain't sure about old Seth Rossiter. He knows I got a hankering to live in Mexico and he just might be laying out along the trail waiting for me."

"It'll be smart to go through Texas, then," the woman agreed absently. Again she brushed at her eyes. "I'm so sleepy I can hardly see! I think I'll doze for a spell while the horses are taking it easy." Pausing, she looked directly at Finley, smiled meaningfully, and added: "I didn't get much sleep last night."

Duke laughed outright, winked broadly. "You go right ahead, catch yourself forty winks. I'll see to your horse keeping up with us—you can bet on that! I sure ain't about to lose you!"

Nella's lips parted briefly again in a worn smile, and closing her eyes, she let her head fall forward. Duke, maneuvering his gray into her mount, crowded it into the center of the road, where, with the two other horses to either side, it would maintain direction and pace without the rider using the reins.

Shortly after midafternoon they reached Bitter Creek—a general store and saloon standing a short distance back from a large stock-watering pond. They halted there only briefly while Finley purchased another bottle of whiskey and the horses slaked their thirsts, and then rode on.

"I'm getting in kind of a rush," Duke, coldly ignoring Ferd Kissler, explained to the now awake Nella when they were again on their way. "Want to grab up that money and light out for the border. The more I hash it about in my noggin, the anxiouser I am for us to get down there and start living like I figure—eating and drinking and taking it easy, and spending a lot of time—"

"Is the next town far?" the woman broke in, glancing ahead.

They were off the broad mesa across which they had been moving, and were now passing between fairly high hills covered with brush, rock, and scattered pines.

"About two days," Finley said a bit impatiently as if weary of her asking much the same question continually. "Place called Longhorn. You needing something special, or you just wanting to know?"

"I'm tired of riding—of this saddle," she said with a long sigh. "And I'm tired of having to sleep on the ground at night, and eating the way we do. I'd like to go to a hotel, get a room, take a hot bath, and—"

Duke jerked a thumb at Kissler. "Was just what I had cooked up for us at Pine Valley, only he went and spoiled it—"

"I know," Nella said hurriedly, apparently wanting to avoid the subject. "But I can wait—I'm strong and I can manage. You'd be surprised at how strong I am."

"Nope, I wouldn't," Duke said. "You're forgetting I've known you for quite a spell—almost ever since you and Rube got hitched. Expect I know about as much about you as he did, in fact, after—"

102

"Is there a hotel in this town where you hid the money?"

Duke pulled off his hat, and letting the gray's reins hang from the saddlehorn, probed his thick dark hair with his fingers.

"Can't recollect saying it was hid in no town," he said. "Howsomever, I'll tell you this much—we sure won't be far from a hotel—a real nice one."

"Then it is in some town."

"Yep, expect I'll have to admit it."

"Mind telling me the name of the place?"

Duke replaced his hat, shook his head. "Now, what'd be the use of me doing that? I'm taking you there and we're getting the money together, ain't we? You keep nagging and prying just like we wasn't in this together. I don't savvy why you're always asking."

"Only one reason, Duke," she replied, smiling tenderly, "for your sake. If something happened to you—an accident—and I had to have cash to help you, I could go and get it."

"Ain't nothing going to happen to me," Finley said. "Not unless I get hit by lightning."

"That's what I mean," the woman said quickly. "You can't be sure of anything. Now, if I knew what town it was that we're going to, and where in it you and Rube hid the money—"

Duke grinned. "You don't want to know that! It just might slip out, because women simply ain't built right to keep secrets—and I sure don't want some jasper like Kissler there hearing about it."

Nella frowned. "Duke, you don't think that I—that Ferd and me—"

"No, I ain't saying you two are in cahoots. You done explained to me how things just sort of took place the other night, and I'm believing it—but you could sort of let it slip out—no more'n a wee bit, mind you—and he could maybe put two and two together and wind up with the answer."

"You don't know me as good as you think you do—"

"Oh, I reckon I do, and just maybe I know women better'n you do. Anyways, there ain't no point in us getting all fired up about it. I aim to keep on like we are—me being the only one that knows where the thirty thousand dollars is stashed, and taking you to it."

Nella Brodie stirred, changed position on her saddle. "You know best," she conceded reluctantly. "But I can see why you want to be careful. It's a lot of money; I hope it's still where you and Rube put it."

"It'll be there," Finley said, glancing to the west.

The sun was almost gone and he knew they should be looking for a spot to make camp. But his spirits were high, and since he was still buoyantly riding the crest that the previous night's activities had carried him to, he didn't feel like stopping. The sooner he retrieved the money, the sooner Nella and he could head for Mexico and begin the new life he was anticipating.

"You mind us riding for a spell?" he asked. The horses were walking, taking one of their periodic breaks from the steady lope they maintained, and conversation was easier.

"No, I guess not. Why?"

"I'm wanting to get to where we're going fast as we can."

Nella's eyes brightened. "That mean we're getting close? You said—"

"It's a ways yet, but was we to keep going a bit longer, it'd shorten it up a bit."

"That would be fine," the woman said resignedly. "We can't get there any too soon to suit me."

Duke Finley beamed with his understanding of her meaning. "Me neither, lady—me neither," he said.

★ 20 ★

Rossiter arrived at Bitter Creek with a light rain shower dimpling the pond that spread, like a dark mirror, nearby.

It could hardly be called a town, was more what was usually termed a wide place in the road, he saw, and reckoned that the general store with its adjacent saloon existed for the accomodation of the cowhands and drovers who stopped at the pond to water the herds they were driving north.

Allowing the sorrel to quench his thirst, and taking the opportunity to refill his canteen, Rossiter rode on to the store and halted at the lengthy hitchrack. A young woman dressed in an ankle-length mother-hubbard dress came out onto the narrow porch and greeted him.

"Pa's in the saloon if you're a-looking for him," she said, pointing to the adjoining structure.

Rossiter said, "Not looking for him—looking for information. Did three people pass through here yesterday, maybe late? Would've been two men and a woman."

The girl nodded. "Was here late, like you're saying."

"They stay over?"

"No, just kept going after buying some liquor."

"North?"

"Yes, sir—headed for Longhorn."

Rossiter gave that thought. Then, "How far's that from here?"

An elderly man appeared in the entrance to the saloon at that moment. Squat, graying, clad in wrinkled blue serge pants, vest, and collarless white shirt, he considered the lawman sourly.

"What's he want, Ellie?"

"Was asking about them folks that was here yesterday afternoon."

The storekeeper pulled back into the doorway slightly in an effort to escape the light shower. "He do any buying?"

"Not yet—"

"Well, we ain't here for our health, mister," the older man said, turning his attention to Rossiter. "You want to ask about something, then you step down and do some buying."

Rossiter reached into a pocket, produced his star, and held it up for the storekeeper to see. "This says I don't have to," he stated, and then dropping it back into its place of concealment, swung from the saddle and moved toward the saloon. "Expect I can use a couple of drinks, however."

The old man withdrew into the building's shadowy interior and circled in behind a makeshift bar.

"What'll it be?"

"Rye whiskey if you've got it."

"Whiskey—that's what I've got."

Rossiter smiled faintly. Plain, everyday, homemade rot gut—that's what it would be. He accepted the shot glass, filled to the brim, tossed off the fiery liquid, and laying a quarter on the counter, shook his head to a refill. One was enough.

"Just right," the saloonman said, picking up the coin. "Now, what was it you was digging out of Ellie?"

Rossiter smiled again. "Wasn't digging—just asking. Last thing I said was how far is it to this Longhorn?"

"Stranger, eh?"

"Through here. Live down in Cherryville. Know that part of the country. This far north is a mite out of my territory."

"Reckon Longhorn's a couple of days ride from here. You chasing them folks on account of they busted the law? Seemed right nice people to me—specially the one called Duke."

Evidently his old saddle partner had lost none of his charm, Rossiter thought as he turned and started for the door. Abruptly he paused, looked back.

"Be a friend of mine showing up here later. Horse went lame on him. I'll be obliged if you'll give him all the help you can. Like as not he'll be needing another horse."

"Ain't nothing to ride around here unless some of the ranch hands drop by."

Rossiter nodded. "Do what you can. I'll make it worth your while when I come back through."

The storekeeper's attitude changed greatly. "Sure, Sheriff," he said, his weathered features at last cracking into the semblance of a smile. "Can depend on me helping him all I can. I sure will!"

Rossiter moved on, stepped out into the open. The shower had ceased, he noted as he crossed to the sorrel and ruefully considered his wet saddle. Cupping his hand, he scooped away the loose drops and swung aboard. The outlaws were now no more than half a day ahead of him, he figured, pointing the big gelding north, and alone now, he could travel fast. A hard glint came into his deep-set eyes; the chase was almost over.

Jubal Seibert halted at the edge of the pond, and letting the buckskin have his way, considered the town of Bitter Creek with a jaundiced eye. Hell, it wasn't a town at all! It was nothing but a saloon and a general store—no livery stable, no blacksmith, no nothing that could satisfy his needs, as far as he could tell. Maybe around back of the place there'd be a barn.

Taking up the buckskin's reins, he pulled the horse away from the water and continued toward the structure, heedless of the scattered mud holes the recent shower had created in low areas.

Reaching the corner of the building, Seibert started around to the rear, pulled up short as the storekeeper abruptly appeared on the porch and advanced to its edge.

"You the man the sheriff said would be coming?"

Jubal gave that thought. "Depends. What was he riding?"

"Sorrel. Never spoke out his name, but he's chasing two men and a woman."

"That's him. Wasn't figuring on being expected. Name's Jubal Seibert. Who're you?"

"John Mason. This here's my place. Me and my granddaughter run it. Sheriff said your horse went lame on you."

"Did, for a fact."

"Sheriff said I was to help you all I could."

"What I'm needing is a horse. Done rode this buckskin too far and too hard and he ain't going to be fit for nothing for a while."

"I ain't got no horses," Mason said, glancing around as his granddaughter came from the store's interior and took a stand by the doorway. "Told the sheriff that."

Jubal swore under his breath and moved forward until he was in the shadow cast by the store building, and out of the sun. The shower earlier had only made the heat worse.

"Well, where am I going to get something to ride, then?" the scout asked, pulling off his old campaign hat and mopping at the sweat on his face. "Sure ought to be somebody around that'll loan or rent me a horse."

"Two or three ranches on to the west of me, but it's a mighty long walk," Mason said. "Smart thing for you to do is just settle down and wait. Like as not there'll be some cowhand ride in tonight or tomorrow looking to spark my granddaughter, or buy hisself a drink, and maybe you can fix it up with him to get you a horse."

Jubal gave that brief thought, nodded. "Reckon I'll just picket old Jim over there by the pond and then come in and have a drink or two—and do some waiting, like you said. I done had all the walking I want for a spell."

"I'll be in the saloon," Mason said, and turned away.

Jubal, accepting his lot without rancor, led the limping buckskin over to the water, and loosening the saddle cinch and slipping the bit, secured the horse to one of the trees that ringed the pond. There wasn't much grass to be grazed—previously passing herds of cattle having cropped it thoroughly—but there were a few new shoots, and no doubt Mason would have some grain in his store with which the buckskin's feed could be supplemented.

He could sure use a little feed himself, Jubal thought as he crossed over and entered the saloon. He'd treat himself to a couple of drinks and then see about some vittles. Maybe John Mason would let him sit at his table for supper. Like as not that young girl he claimed was his granddaughter was a good cook.

"You wanting whiskey?" Mason greeted as the one-time army guide stepped up to the bar. "Or maybe you'd like some Mex tequila. It'll sure rattle your whiskers—"

"You got some beer?" Seibert asked. "I'm needing something wet—and cool."

"Sure, I got beer but it ain't no cooler than it is under the floor—that being where I keep it."

"Be fine. Expect you best figure on three or four glasses if it's a chore to draw it," Jubal said, and then thinking again about the possibility of a good woman-cooked meal, added, "Just you have one yourself—on me."

Mason, bending over behind his plank bar as he opened a small trapdoor in the floor, paused, glanced up.

"Why, sure, I'd be mighty pleased to," he said.

The soft thud of hoofs out in front of the building drew Jubal Seibert's attention. He turned, padded softly for the door. It could be a cowhand from one of the ranches Mason had mentioned, or—the realization came swiftly—it could be the pilgrim who had been dogging his and Seth Rossiter's trail for so many days.

Reaching the saloon's entrance, Jubal halted, frowned. The rider, stocky, dark hair crowding out from under his hat, was dismounting. It was the pilgrim, he was certain, for he didn't have the look of a cowpuncher. At that moment the man wheeled and looked up.

Jubal's jaw sagged. "You!" he shouted. "It's been you a-following us! Why the hell—"

For answer the rider drew his pistol and fired. Seibert rocked back on his heels, staggered, and fell forward.

"You!" he gasped again. "Why—"

But the rider had hurriedly swung back onto his horse, cut sharply about, and was racing off up the trail—north.

★ 21 ★

"I reckon you see now that I knew what I was talk-ing about when I said I'd lose the sheriff," Duke said when they halted to breathe the horses.

They had been riding fast in accordance with his wish to reach the money stash as soon as possible, and the pace was now beginning to tell not only on their mounts but on Nella and Kissler as well. Duke, accus-tomed to hard riding, was showing little of the effect.

"Was that trick back there at that springs," he con-tinued, staring off over the country they had just cov-ered. "Expect old Seth's still heading for Fort Worth."

Nella wiped at her face with a small handkerchief. She appeared wan and near exhaustion. Her clothing, dirt-streaked from dust, rain, and sweat, hung like rags from her small frame, and there was an impatient glint in her dark eyes.

"I hope so—" she murmured.

"Hope! There ain't no doubt about it! That's where he is—somewhere in Texas by now. We've seen the last of Seth Rossiter. But, you know, it kind of makes me feel bad, making a fool of him like I've done—but there just weren't no getting around it."

"Counting your chips before the game's over, ain't you, cowboy?" Kissler commented dryly.

He had the nugget of green jade that he wore suspended from his neck, between a thumb and forefinger and was rubbing it absently.

"We're a long ways from getting that money—and he just might show up at any time," the gambler added.

"Well, now, maybe it ain't as far as you figure," Duke shot back.

"You keep telling us that but we don't ever get there. I'm beginning to think this ain't nothing but a snipe hunt—that there never was thirty thousand dollars— that you're just stringing Nella along so's you can be with her!"

Duke's eyes flared with anger. He glanced at the woman. She was studying him narrowly, speculatively.

"You thinking that, too?" he demanded.

Nella shrugged. "Does seem like it's taking us a long time to get there. Maybe, if you'd tell us exactly where it is you and Rube hid—"

"Not a chance!" Duke cut in flatly. "That's something I'm keeping in my head till we get there."

"Which is the same as saying you don't trust me," Nella said stiffly. "That's pretty hard to understand after what you and me've been to each other, and considering all the plans we've made."

"I don't trust your necklace-wearing friend there, that's who I don't trust!" Duke shouted. "And you ought to be thanking me for being like I am about it instead of ragging me all the time. I'm being real careful and looking out for us and not taking no chances."

"Chances? What chances would you be taking?"

"Of getting my throat cut when I'm sleeping, or maybe getting shot in the back while I'm riding along. That's about what'd happen to me if he knew where the cash was."

"Ferd wouldn't try that, not with me around."

"Maybe not, but you ain't around all the time, and anyways, I don't see how you could stop him."

Kissler, sitting silently by, thumbs now hooked in the lower pockets of his leather vest, smiled faintly. "You're talking about me like I was over in the next county instead of right here, listening. What you both better know is I'm no killer—not even when the stakes are thirty thousand dollars. Money just ain't worth all that much to me."

"Yeh, I'll bet not," Duke said derisively. "I ain't never seen the man yet, specially the gambling kind, that wouldn't steal from his blind grandma!"

Kissler hawked, spat. "That so? Well, you're looking at one now—and you're looking at a man, too, that's got mighty damn tired of this kind of talk! I want to know one thing, and I want a straight answer—when do we get to where you cached that money?"

Duke grinned. "Thought I heard you saying that money don't mean nothing to you?"

"I did, but I've been tied down with this mess for a month and I've got to make some plans. I need to know when I'll be getting paid off and where I'll be when I do. Can figure then where to go."

"It make a difference? I always figured a cardsharp could go anywhere there was a saloon and find hisself a game."

Kissler ignored the slur. "I'll be looking for a big game—one where I can win a lot of money."

"I can see Ferd's point," Nella said. "We ought to tell him what he wants to know so that he can make his plans."

Duke, gaze again reaching out over the rolling hills to the high mountains in the east, gave that thought.

"I'll think on it," he said after a time, and squaring himself in his saddle, added, "Let's move out."

Nella and Kissler lifted their reins and swung in beside him, the woman to his right and abreast, Ferd Kissler on the left and a bit behind.

For a full hour as they rode steadily northward on a wide, definite trail that lay between grassy slopes to either side, Finley gave his problem consideration. About them the day was bright and clear, with no sign of more rain in the sky. Jays whipped erratically in and out of the trees, the bright blue of their feathers flashing in the sunlight, and patches of yellow and purple flowers on the hillsides broke the sameness of the sage-green ground cover.

"What about it?" Kissler asked finally. "You got your mind made up yet?"

"I reckon I'll speak out when I'm damn good and ready," Duke snapped, his attitude of near friendliness to the gambler abruptly disappearing, to be replaced by the cold tolerance that had characterized their relationship. "I sure ain't owing you nothing!"

Nella threw a quick glance at Ferd, said disapprovingly, "Now, don't crowd Duke. He's smart enough to know what's best. I expect he'll tell you what you want to know just as soon as he gets things sorted out."

Duke nodded, smiled at the woman. "That's right. I know what's best."

Ferd leaned forward on his saddle, eased himself by standing in the stirrups. "I ain't saying you don't—and you're the boss, for certain—but it'll sure help me a-plenty was I to know where I'll be and what I'll be doing a week from now.

"Different with you and Nella. You'll be on your way to Mexico and making big plans for what you're going to do when you get there. But me—hell, I can't make no plans."

"I'll tell you this much," Finley said grudgingly. "Come tonight, we'll be reaching Longhorn."

"That a town?"

"Yeh, we'll be staying there—it's got a real fine hotel and restaurant. Then about two days later we'll be riding into another town—Saddlerock."

The eyes of both Nella and Ferd were on Duke, expectant, hopeful.

"That's where we're headed for—Saddlerock."

"You mean that's where the money's hidden?" the woman asked, staring intently at him.

"That's the place," Duke said. "Now, I ain't saying where in Saddlerock, but it'll be far as we'll have to go. Now, Mister Necklace-Wearing Man, you know where you'll be when you collect your pay. Go ahead and do your planning and don't rag me no more about it!"

Ferd Kissler settled back in his saddle, a satisfied look in his pale eyes. "Obliged to you, Duke. That sure takes a load off my mind."

★ 22 ★

Seth Rossiter rode into Longhorn with a worn,
nearly exhausted sorrel horse under him, but they had
covered many miles that day and no doubt had gained
on the outlaws.

As he turned into the settlement he glanced back,
with the hope that Jubal Seibert, despite his continual
objections and complaining, would be in sight and
coming on—but he had little faith that such would be
the case; Jubal would find no help in Bitter Creek. His
one chance of finding a mount to replace the buckskin
would be a rancher or a cowhand happening by—and
that was a long shot.

But there was a lone rider well behind him—the pilgrim on the dark-colored horse they had been seeing
almost from the time they had ridden out of Cherryville. The lawman wondered if Seibert had endeavored to talk him out of his mount when the two
had finally met, either borrowing or buying the animal,
and decided that the old scout probably had tried. Jubal
might be a bellyacher but he was no quitter and would
do his utmost to catch up.

The pilgrim, as before, was still a barely discernible
figure, never drawing closer or losing ground, but

maintaining a set, distance, as if it had been prescribed. Who he was and what he had in mind was a puzzle nagging at Rossiter's mind, and he wished several times that he could pull up, wait, and see what it was all about.

The lawman went immediately to the livery stable at the far end of Longhorn's main street, and while himself tired, spent some time with the hostler going over the sorrel, examining his hoofs, shoes, and giving him a brisk rubdown. After he had seen with his own eyes that a proper feeding of grain and clean hay was made, and that the big gelding had received all the attention possible to put him in condition for another hard day, which would come only too soon, he started back to the street, and the hotel.

"Aim to be pulling out an hour or so before first light," he said, pausing in the doorway. "You be around or had I best pay you now?"

"Pay me now," the hostler said. "Be a dollar and a half."

Rossiter counted out the prescribed amount, again turned to go to the hotel, and once more hesitated. He knew the answer to the question he intended to ask, but being a thorough man not inclined to taking matters for granted, he voiced it, nevertheless.

"Three people—two men and a woman—I'm trying to overtake them. Probably stayed here last night and rode out this morning. You see them?"

"Reckon I did. They done just what you said— stayed the night, rode north. Was around nine o'clock, I expect."

"Obliged," the lawman said, and moved on.

He wasn't as near to the outlaws as he'd thought, he realized, but he was now aware, definitely, of just how far behind he was. Another day or two, traveling alone and fast, as he was, and he'd be right on their heels— and the time would be at hand to decide just how he would handle the situation. He would be up against two desperate men and an equally dangerous woman.

With Jubal siding him it wouldn't have been so difficult; alone it would be a risky chore. Of course, if Duke and Brodie had hidden the money in or near a town where there was a lawman, he could recruit assistance. There was no way of knowing about anything, however, until the time came.

Reaching the hotel, Rossiter registered for a room under the curious eyes of a young clerk who wanted to talk but gave it up when his comments evoked no responses from the weary, grim-faced lawman.

Going immediately to his quarters, Rossiter stripped off, washed himself down with water from a bowl filled from the tin pitcher, and then feeling a bit less tired but still hungry, returned to the street, where a dozen or so residents were strolling about in the evening coolness, and sought out a restaurant.

Conscious that the next day and possibly the following would be ones during which he would be traveling fast and likely unwilling to halt even for coffee, he ordered a big supper of steak, potatoes, and all the trimmings, leisurely downed it, and then retraced his steps to the hotel, where he immediately went to bed.

Aroused by an inner awakening system, he was up, dressed, and at the livery stable well before first light. The doors of the barn were closed but unlocked, and entering, he went to the sorrel's stall, saddled and bridled him, and rode out a brief half hour later.

The air was crisp and clear, and the sky bending overhead still showed stars, although there were a few smudgy areas which indicated the presence of rain clouds yet hanging about. The gelding, after the night's rest and feeding, was at his best and set his own pace along the trail at a fast lope.

Late in the afternoon Rossiter came to a crossroads. There was no settlement or even a store or saloon such as there had been back at Harper's Springs or Bitter

Creek—only a faded sign, half down, that named the intersection as Skull Crossing.

Coming off his saddle, the lawman examined the trail carefully. Duke could have turned east, headed for the high mountains that loomed blue-gray in the distance, or he could have swung west for the low hill country and one of the settlements or ranches that he assumed were in that area. And he could as easily have continued north.

Here was one of the times when he badly needed Jubal Seibert, but the old scout was not there and he could only use his own powers of observation and logic and determine for himself which direction the outlaws had taken.

The north road was hard-packed and studded with rocks. Rossiter thought he found several markings on some of the stones—ones left by contact from iron horseshoes—but he could not convince himself that they were recently made.

But by the same token the loose dust on the east and west forks of the trail revealed no hoofprints whatever. Cleared by the recent rain showers, they were perfectly smooth. Duke and the others could only have continued north, the lawman finally concluded, and settling on that, resumed his course.

Not long after that, Rossiter noted dust some distance to the west and judged, from the amount of it, that a cattle drive was underway to some point east of him. And then later, around noon, he caught sight of the pilgrim again. The man appeared to be a bit nearer, but it could have been an illusion brought about by the clearness of the day.

Rossiter studied the far-away figure briefly, wishing as before that it would be Jubal Seibert hurrying to overtake him on a fresh horse, but realizing, even as he hoped, that it could not be since time and miles would make it an impossibility.

It could only be the pilgrim, persistent, puzzling, and

thoroughly infuriating. Why the hell didn't the man either turn off or catch up? Why did he hang back, seemingly unwilling to make known his identity? It was like having someone standing just outside your camp at night, watching, keeping just beyond the reach of the firelight, and never letting you see him, the lawman thought. Dammit to hell, if he wasn't in such a hurry he'd pull off into the brush alongside the trail, wait, and teach that heel-dogging jasper some manners when he arrived!

After a long day, Rossiter camped that night beside a small spring, laying his blanket and picketing the sorrel well back in the underbrush. He did this not in fear of some passerby but because the soft mud around the spring indicated that it was a water hole—probably the only one within miles—frequented by deer, cougar, wolves, and the other wild things. If he had camped too close, his presence would have prevented them from fulfilling their needs.

He awoke near first light to the sound of the wind rushing through the trees and rattling the brush, and being no stranger in a land where such was not uncommon, he prepared himself for a disagreeable day, all the while hoping the wind, dry with dust and sand, would lay with the coming of the sun.

But it did not, and by midmorning had developed into a full-strength duster blowing in from the panhandle. It soon slowed the sorrel's pace and necessitated halting periodically so that the lawman could swab the big gelding's nostrils and lips and wipe his eyes with a rag wet with water from the canteen.

He was losing time—but there was no help for it, Rossiter realized. He could only hope the wind would stop soon.

★ 23 ★

"Saddlerock—three miles," Nella said.

She was holding a handkerchief to her face in an effort to block out as much of the blowing sand and dust as possible while she read the canted sign standing at the side of the trail. Abruptly she turned to Duke.

"Didn't you tell us that it was Saddlerock where you and Rube hid the money?"

Finley grinned. They had fought the fierce wind all day and his teeth were gritty, his eyes red-rimmed and inflamed, but such in no way dimmed the triumph of the moment for him.

"I sure did, lady! This here's the place!"

Ferd Kissler, hat pulled low on his head, moved up beside the woman. Eyes squinted, he endeavored to look beyond, get a glimpse of the settlement, but the air was filled with a tan pall and visibility was limited to less than a hundred yards.

"Hell, let's keep going," he said, raising his voice to be heard above the howl of the wind. "No sense setting out here in this damned cyclone when we could be inside."

"This here little breeze bothering you, Mister Necklace Man?" Duke asked chidingly. "Why, this ain't hardly nothing! I've seen the dirt coming in off the panhandle so danged thick a man on a horse couldn't tell if he was looking backward or forward unless he—"

"Can't we go on into town?" Nella interrupted. Her lifted voice had a desperate pitch to it as she clung to the lapels of her jacket with one hand in an effort to prevent its being ripped from her body, while she continued to hold the handkerchief to her face with the other. "I—I can't stand any more of this—of this dirt and wind—"

"Sure," Duke replied. "And it won't be so bad down in town—it kind of being in a big hollow. We can go right straight to Dora's—she's an old friend of mine—have ourselves something to drink and eat. It's most noon—dinner time."

Nella nodded, raised her eyes to the sky in quest of the sun. It was a pale, silver-looking ball beyond a transparent yellow curtain. "It's a while yet till noon. Won't it be best to get the money first—be sure it's still there?"

Duke spat the grit from his mouth, grinned. "It'll be there—don't you fret."

He was enjoying himself, his time of supremacy, despite the ravaging elements. He was the one completely in command now, even more so than he had been during the long journey from Cherryville, and he was making the most of it. Seeing both Nella and Ferd Kissler hanging on to each word he said, and utterly dependent upon him now for every move, pleased him beyond belief. And his importance would increase as time wore on, Duke realized, and in the interests of such, he reckoned he'd stall just a bit more, stretch things out as much as possible.

"Hell, there ain't no big hurry," he said, raking his horse with his spurs and starting him down the grade. "Just set back, take it real easy."

At once Nella and Kissler moved in beside him, and

protesting no more, rode down the long slope into the broad valley in which Saddlerock lay.

Reaching the edge of the settlement, Duke swung in behind an abandoned adobe hut that stood a bit off to the side and that offered shelter from the driving wind. Although the wind was a little less violent than it had been higher up on the trail, there was no decrease in the volume of dust and sand that it carried.

"Pretty good-looking little town, ain't it?" Finley said, gesturing at the dozen or so buildings that were lined, shoulder to shoulder, along the north side of the town's one street. There was nothing opposite them— even the few residences and the small white steepled church were set apart and to the east.

"What're we stopping here for?" Ferd demanded, wiping at his mouth. "If we ain't going to where you hid the money, then lets get the hell inside one of them saloons!"

Duke glanced at Nella, still taking full enjoyment from every passing moment. "Now, what do you say, lady? You in a big hurry?"

Nella Brodie nodded helplessly. "Please, Duke, get me out of this terrible dust and wind, and sand!"

"Sure thing," Finley said, relenting, and moving off away from the minimal shelter the old adobe hut had offered, led the way into the street and to a saloon near the west end of the weathered structures.

"This here's Dora's place," he said, pulling up to the rack fronting a narrow storeroom. Two small windows faced the street and both were covered with what appeared to be saddle blankets. The door, of solid wood, was closed.

"You sure this friend of yours is open?" Nella said doubtfully, starting to loosen the scarf she had placed over her hat and tied beneath her chin as a means for keeping it from blowing away. "It certainly doesn't look—"

"She's open," Duke assured her. "It's always this

way when the danged wind comes in from the panhandle. Whole town just sort of buttons up and sets back and waits till it's over. Just ain't much else folks can do."

"We leaving the horses here?" Ferd asked, coming off his saddle.

Duke smiled. "Well, we ain't going to be needing them—leastwise, not till we're ready to move on. I reckon it'd be a good thing was you to take them around back. Hotel's got a stable there."

The gambler frowned, swore deeply. "Why don't we ride them—"

"Mostly because I'm telling you to take them," Duke cut in flatly, a hard grin on his dirt-streaked face.

Kissler drew up stiffly but relented as he caught a warning glance from the woman. Shrugging, he gathered in the reins of the three horses and started for the corner.

"We'll be inside, waiting," Duke shouted after him, and taking Nella by the arm, stepped up onto the board sidewalk. Pushing the woman before him, their heads bowed to the wind, he opened the door to the saloon and they entered.

The room was dimly lit by two sooted chimney lamps bracketed to the walls. There was a warm stuffiness to the place, which was filled with the smells of tobacco smoke, spilled whiskey, and sweat. A pale aura of fine dust hung in the air. Two men were hunched over the bar, behind which stood a large, beefy, red-faced woman with close-cropped gray hair.

"Howdy, Dora," Duke greeted. "We'll be needing some grub—three plates—and a bottle of your best whiskey."

The two patrons roused long enough to look Duke and the woman over and then resumed their inactivity. Dora, finishing off the drink she was holding in a thick-fingered hand, set the glass down and came out from back of the counter.

"Find yourself a table over there," she directed, pointing vaguely to the rear of the room. All the time that she was speaking in a deep raspy voice, she was eyeing Duke Finley closely as if endeavoring to remember him. "You say three plates of vittles? I don't count but two of you."

"Be another man along in a minute. I sent him around to the stable with the horses," Duke explained, selecting a table in the corner.

"That's good," Dora said. "Ain't fit for man or beast to be out on a day like this. Reckon it's about the worst blow we've had in years. . . . You want your whiskey now?"

"Yep, and three glasses. You got a place where my woman can sort of wash up a mite? We been riding in that wind and dust all day."

Dora smiled down at Nella. "Sure have, long as she don't mind coming out to the kitchen. Got a pump and a wash pan there. How about yourself?"

"Expect I can wait till we get to the hotel—"

"So will I," Nella said quickly. Her shoulders stirred wearily. "I'm too tired right now to do anything but sit."

Dora wheeled, crossed to the bar, and returned immediately with a bottle of whiskey and the required number of glasses.

"This here'll fix you up, honey," she said, placing a glass in front of Nella and filling it to the brim. "Wind like that just beats a body to death. . . . You ready to eat now?"

Duke had removed his jacket, loosened his shirt collar, and now beyond reach of the wind, was beginning to relax. Nella was following his example.

"Yeh, might as well," he said, and glanced to the door as it swung in, admitting Ferd Kissler and a gritty blast. "Here comes our friend now. You can bring all three plates."

"You be wanting coffee, too?"

125

"Sure—only don't go bringing none of that damn chicory! We want the real thing."

"Ain't never served no chicory yet," Dora declared angrily and thumped heavily off toward a door at the back of the room, which led, no doubt, to the kitchen.

"You get them horses all comfortable like?" Duke asked as Ferd sank onto one of the chairs and began to take off his coat.

Kissler nodded. "They'll be all right. Told the hostler we'd not be needing them today—maybe tomorrow."

"Yeh, maybe tomorrow," Duke said, filling the glasses. Raising his, he eyed it appraisingly. "This sure is going to taste mighty welcome!" he added, and tossed off the whiskey.

"What's that mean—maybe tomorrow?" Ferd asked, holding his drink. "If we go get that money today, we sure can be gone—"

"If we get it today," Duke echoed tauntingly, accenting the first word. "Just might decide to go to the hotel first—me and Nella. She's wanting to clean up a bit, and I—"

"That can wait!" Nella cut in. "I'm not that anxious to wash off—and I'm really not all that tired."

"Meaning," Finley said coyly, "you're for going and getting the money first off—"

Nella's lips formed a snap reply, but she choked it back, forced a patient smile. "I think it would be best, Duke. Once we get it—have it in our hands—then we can all quit worrying."

"Worrying? Who's worrying?" Duke wanted to know.

The woman shrugged. "You know what I mean. We're not even sure it's still there—wherever it was you hid it. Somebody might have found it."

"Nope, it'll be there," Finley stated confidently, and looked around as Dora, carrying three plates heaped with steaming stew, approached.

"I'll go get your coffee and some bread—made it fresh this morning," the big woman said, placing the plates before them. Reaching into the pocket of her apron, she produced knives, forks, and spoons, and laid them beside the plates. "You all go ahead, start. I'll be right back."

"How long're you aiming to hang around here?" Ferd asked finally, in a falling voice, and then downed his drink.

"Couple, three hours," Duke replied lightly, taking up his fork and beginning to eat. "There just ain't no hurry. I ain't never yet seen a double-eagle with legs that could up and walk off."

★ 24 ★

The faded sign, weathered by years and barely legible in the closing, dust-filled darkness, had said: SADDLEROCK—3 MILES. Rossiter had not halted as he puzzled out the words, but continued riding, looking forward eagerly to reaching the settlement and getting in out of the relentless, punishing wind.

It looked to be a town like most all others. A single row of buildings lining one side of a street—three or four saloons, a store, a meat market, a hotel with but one floor, a few vacant structures, and a large livery stable. The homes of the residents, and their church, were on beyond, as if desiring to be disassociated from the bleak, wind-scoured business buildings.

Neckerchief pulled up over his nose and mouth to ward off the dust and stinging sand, the lawman entered the end of the street and proceeded past the structures—all closed tight and looking abandoned—toward the stables. He was thoughtfully speculating as to what Duke and his friends, upon reaching the settlement under present conditions, would have done.

Logically, they would have halted and sought shelter from the weather, as they likely had fought the wind for all that day just as he had. Too, their horses would be in need of rest and thus it was only reasonable to believe they had halted to wait out the savage blow—assuming, of course, that he had been near enough to overtake them.

He wished now that he'd had the foresight to circle the town and come into the livery barn from the rear. Duke, if he was there, just might have seen him riding down the street if he happened to be looking out of a window somewhere along the way. But moments later the lawman dismissed that fear. Each of the buildings had some sort of cover over its windows in an attempt to turn back the dust and sand. The odds that Duke would pull aside one of the drapes and glance out at the very moment of his passing were far too long—if the outlaws were there at all.

Rossiter came to the livery barn, pulled up before its wide doors. Both were shut tight. Riding in close, he hammered on one with a boot heel. After a bit of a delay it opened enough to admit him and the sorrel, and sighing gratefully, he rode on in. Halting in the runway, the lawman came stiffly off the saddle, nodded to the hostler—a tall, lank man with a tobacco-stained beard and mustache.

"Sure ain't no day for joy-riding," the stablekeeper said. "Name's Giffy. You staying the night?"

"Not sure," Rossiter said, glancing down the line of empty stalls. "Am I your only customer?"

"The only pilgrim," Giffy said. "Got me a few regulars in the back. You expecting somebody?"

"Two men and a woman. Sort of figured they'd be here."

The hostler wagged his head, paused to listen as some kind of commotion took place in a rear stall, and then said, "Well, they sure ain't come into my place yet, mister. That mean you'll be riding on?"

The lawman gave that thought. Was it possible Duke and the others had gone on? We're they farther ahead of him than he figured? Those were questions

129

he'd have to do some puzzling over before deciding what to do next.

"Not right away," Rossiter said wearily. "Like for you to look after my horse just the same, however. Clean out his mouth and nostrils and feed and water him while I go get a bite of supper. If it works out that I'll have to move on, I'll be back for him."

Giffy shook his head. "Man's a dang fool to get out in this—unless he just has to."

"That's just it," the lawman said, turning and heading for the door. Somewhere outside the building a shutter was flapping wildly, the sound of its hammering against a wall echoing throughout the low-roofed building. "I might just have to. . . . There any best place to eat here in Saddlerock?"

"Hotel," the hostler said. "Won't be no big fancy meal, but it'll be clean and not like that slop you'd get at Dora's and some of them other places."

"Dora's," Rossiter repeated, raising his voice to be heard as he opened one of the doors. "Saw the sign when I rode in. Saloon?"

"Yeh—"

"Never take my meals in a saloon unless I have to," the lawman said, and stepped out into the howling night.

Head down, feeling the sting of sand, the buffeting of the wind, he walked slowly toward the center of the row of structures where he had noted the hotel. He'd do a bit of checking there, too, see if Duke and his friends had signed in for the night. If not, the answer was clear; the outlaws had not stopped over, and despite the storm—which unquestionably had been raging when they were there—had continued on their way.

For where? The next town, as he recalled, was Capital City itself—a long two-day ride, with no settlement in between. It didn't seem reasonable—the storm being

130

what it was and after bracing it for hours—that they would ride on. Unless—

Reaching the hotel, Seth Rossiter halted. Quickly opening the door, he stepped hurriedly inside to minimize the inrush of wind, and as hastily closed it. Placing his shoulders to the panel, he considered the thought that had come into his mind; *unless they were not going far—a few miles, perhaps, to some certain place close by where the money was hidden.*

That could be it, the lawman concluded, and crossed to a short counter behind which an elderly woman awaited him with obvious patience.

"You want a room?" she asked, pushing a register book and pencil at him.

"Not sure I'll be staying over yet," Rossiter said. "Aim to eat a bite in your restaurant, then decide."

The woman, whose lined face reflected disappointment at first, brightened slightly. "We'd just about closed the restaurant down, business being what it is, but I reckon my daughter can fix you up with some supper. Just go on in and set yourself down."

Rossiter nodded. "What's on north of here—on the road to Capital City? There a town?"

"Nope," the hotel woman said. "Now, there's a crossroads—place with a saloon and little two-bit store, but that's all. Ain't nobody living around it 'cepting the folks that run it."

"I see. How far's that?"

"Fifteen mile, thereabouts. Best you make up your mind to stay right here tonight. I reckon they could put you up at the crossroads, but if'n they already had a customer, you'd have to sleep on the floor."

"Don't sound like much of a place," the lawman said, and started for the doorway that led into the adjoining restaurant area. Reaching there, he paused, looked back.

"Sort of expected to find some folks I know here.

Were ahead of me on the trail and I figured they'd hole up here till the wind quit. Two men and a woman—"

The woman was shaking her head before he had finished. "Ain't been nobody come in all day."

"There any other place in town where they could get rooms?"

"Nope, this here's the only one. I don't sell groceries and clothes and such, and none of them rents out rooms. That way we stay out of the other fellow's hair."

"Good system," Rossiter commented idly, and walked on into the restaurant.

The area was dimly lit, but as he took a chair at a table well back from the window where a fine haze of dust hung motionless, a girl came through a door in the rear, and striking a match, lit two more of the several lamps that were positioned about the room. Then, with the additional soft light filling the room, she moved up to Rossiter and smiled.

"Steak and beans—that's what we've got today. There's cornbread and honey, and fresh butter. Coffee."

"Suits me," the lawman said indifferently.

He didn't particularly care much what the meal might consist of. He had more riding to do—that had become apparent if he was to lay Duke Finley and his outlaw friends by the heels. He would as soon lay over, wait out the windstorm, and he reckoned he would if it was someone else besides Duke Finley that he was after.

Logic convinced him that Duke was nearby—most likely at the crossroads, fifteen miles north, thus he felt he couldn't risk delaying until morning to resume the pursuit. It made sense; Duke and the others wouldn't have continued in the teeth of such a storm unless they expected their journey to be a short one.

And the fact that one member of the outlaw party was a woman made such reasoning all the more believable. She would have been in the saddle many hours, also, and the blowing dust and sand and the buffeting gusts of wind would have taken their toll of her strength.

The girl reappeared, bringing Rossiter his meal. Taking up knife and fork, the lawman began to eat immediately. He finished quickly, rose, and paying his check, returned to the street.

There had been no letup of the wind, and as he made his way through the darkness for the livery stable, it hammered and whipped at him relentlessly, filling the night around him with the loud slap of loose boards, the rattle of doors and windows, and the squealing of a metal sign somewhere swinging violently back and forth.

Catching Duke Finley and the pair with him, however, would be worth braving the storm—or even one much worse, if that was possible—and he reckoned he was about to accomplish that very thing.

He'd get the sorrel—cleaned, rested some, and fed by now—mount up, and ride to the crossroads. There he'd find Duke and his outlaw partners. Putting chains on them was going to be mighty pleasant.

★ 25 ★

Duke Finley pushed back his chair and beckoned to Dora, standing behind the bar where she was serving several customers. It was full dark, but the wind, despite what everyone had hoped, had failed to subside at sundown and was still flogging the town mercilessly.

Dora, finished, crossed to the table and nodded curtly to Duke. He had been something of a nuisance to her during the time he and his friends had been there.

"What d'you want now?" she demanded.

"Time to be paying up, old gal!" Finley said grandly, and tossed a gold eagle onto the table. "This here's all your'n for the eating and drinking—if you'll do me one more favor."

The big woman shrugged her thick shoulders, picked up the coin. "What's the favor?"

"I'm needing to borrow a lantern."

Dora turned without comment, made her way to the kitchen. She returned shortly with the desired item and handed it to him.

"This all you're wanting?"

Duke bobbed. "Sure is," he said, shaking the lantern. "It full of oil?"

"Was filled this morning."

134

"That's fine. Me and my friends here'll be needing it," Duke said, and taking the bottle of whiskey—the second one purchased since sitting down to eat—got to his feet.

Nella, casting a relieved look at Ferd Kissler, rose. The gambler also drew himself upright, and together they followed Finley to the door. Hanging the bale of the lantern on the crook of an arm, Duke opened the panel, stepped out into the wild night, and paused. Nella and Kissler crowded up close to him.

"Where we going?" the woman shouted.

"Now, just where the hell you figure we're going?" Duke said. "We're going where what we come here for's hid, that's where!"

Ferd smiled tightly at Nella, faced Finley. "You want me to get the horses?"

"Nope, ain't no need," Duke replied, and head down against the wind, started up the street. At once Nella and Kissler moved in beside him.

They walked the length of the dark, windy street, past the hotel and small shops—all closed—crossed the front of the livery stable and the empty store building adjacent to it, and halted, finally, at the last structure in the row—a small wood and tarpaper shack. Handing the bottle of whiskey to Nella, Duke raised his foot and drove it against the door. It burst inward with a splintering sound and the squeal of dry hinges.

"Is this where you and Rube hid all that money?" Nella asked in an awed voice as Finley stepped into the black interior of the shack. Apparently it was unbelievable to her that the two men could have risked so much in such a flimsy place.

Duke, in the center of the room, dust swirling about him while loose boards rattled and banged outside on the roof and walls, tripped the lantern's globe, fired a match with a thumbnail and lit the wick. Light immediately flooded the small cubicle, which contained a makeshift table with benches at each side and two bunks built in one corner.

"Shut that damn door!" Duke yelled at Kissler, setting the lantern on the table. "Enough dirt in here now to plant corn without letting in more."

Ferd closed the warped panel. The lock had broken under Duke's boot, and to hold it tight against its frame, the gambler dragged up one of the benches and wedged it between floor and knob.

"How you like this place?" Duke asked, gesturing at the room in general. "Real cosy, ain't it?"

"Did you really hide all that money—thirty thousand dollars—in this shack?" Nella asked, still finding it hard to believe.

"Sure did. Old Rube cashed in laying right there on that bottom bunk, but before he did I hid the money."

"Where?" Ferd asked, glancing about. "I can't see no place where—"

"And you ain't going to," Duke cut in, taking a pull at the bottle of liquor. "Nobody can. Only me and Rube knows where it is—and he's deader'n a doornail."

Nella moved across to one of the benches and sat down. Dust covered everything with a quarter-inch-thick coating, but she ignored it and the restless tan clouds drifting about, seemed lost in thought as she stared at the narrow bed where her husband had died.

"Wasn't you scared some drifter'd get in, run into the money accidental like?" the gambler wondered. "Or fire—what if somebody'd set fire to the place and burnt it down?"

"Nope, sure wasn't. I locked up tight—and nobody, for sure, was just going to run across it."

"But what if it had burnt down?" Kissler persisted, shaking his head. "This shack'd go up like gunpowder!"

For a long minute there was only the wild sound of the wind howling about the shack and the loud rattle of a board finally coming loose, and then Duke grinned. "Fire'd never get my money. It's buried—under the floor."

Nella came out of her reverie, turned her face, dust-smudged and haggard from long days and nights on the trail, to Finley. "Is that really where it is?"

Duke took another drink, returned the bottle to its place alongside the lantern on the table. "Yep, that's right where it is. Now, you just set back easy and I'll fetch it."

Ferd Kissler, moving to the bench on the opposite side of the table from Nella, settled down, an expectant look on his usually stolid features. The woman, eyes bright, lips slightly parted, hands clasped in her lap, watched intently as Finley crossed to a corner of the room where a scorched and darkened area on the floor indicated the place where a stove had once stood.

Squatting, his thick-bladed knife in hand, the outlaw began to pry at a plank near the wall. It gave after a bit, screeching dryly as he raised it. Laying it aside, Duke reached down through the hole.

"You needing the lantern?" Kissler asked.

Finley shook his head. "Nope," he replied, and began to dig with the knife. "I'm knowing right where the box'll be without having to look."

Abruptly his thrusts with the blade stopped. He grinned, fumbled about in the hole for a few moments, and then, still on his knees, turned and held up a metal cash box of the type commonly used in banks.

"Here y'are—thirty thousand dollars!" he said exultantly, and coming to his feet, returned to the table. "Was right where I put it—just like I kept telling you."

Nella's dark eyes were glowing. "Open it, open it!" she said in a breathless voice. "I've got to see—"

Grinning, Duke released the catch on the container's lid, and leaning over, dumped its contents of currency and coins onto the dusty surface of the table.

"There y'are! That's what thirty thousand dollars looks like!" he said triumphantly.

The woman reached out, began to run her fingers through the loose bills and coins. "All gold and paper—no silver," she murmured. "Why?"

"Me and Rube didn't fool with no silver," Finley said. "Too heavy and don't count for much. Was greenbacks and gold we was after—and sure as hell got!"

"Did, for a fact," Ferd said quietly. He was leaning forward, colorless eyes fixed on the money. His features were expressionless—blank, as if hypnotized.

"Been some folks that wasn't for certain I had thirty thousand dollars stashed away," Duke said pointedly.

"I wasn't one! I never doubted you!" Nella said hurriedly, beginning to make little stacks of the gold eagles. "Never once!"

"What about you, Mister Necklace Man?" Duke said, putting his attention on Kissler. "Seems I recollect you saying a few times—"

"I'm here, ain't I?" Kissler broke in stiffly, coming out of his state of paralysis. "If I hadn't figured you was talking straight, I'd never have come this far."

Duke shrugged, took a turn at the whiskey, and rubbed his palms together. Outside, the wind ripped and tore at the old shack with unbridled ferocity.

"Well, I reckon we best get busy divvying up," he said. "First off, I reckon I'd better pay you what you got coming, Mister Necklace, then you can get the hell out of here and go wherever you're aiming to go. Was twenty-five hundred dollars, Nella said."

"That was her deal," the gambler said quietly, and gun suddenly in hand, he came to his feet. "It ain't mine. I'm taking it all."

Duke Finley drew back, a scowl on his face as he looked closely at Ferd and at the pistol leveled at him. Nearby, Nella had also risen, and frowning, was staring at Kissler.

"Ferd—I—" she began, but he waved her to silence.

"Put all that money back in the box," he directed. "Then shove it across the table to me."

The woman hurriedly collected the bills and the gold eagles, returned them to the container, and closing the lid, pushed it toward the gambler. "Ferd—I never thought you—"

"Now, I'm going out that door," the gambler said, picking up the box. "Either one of you makes a move to follow me, I'll blow your head off—"

"You ain't going nowheres!" Duke yelled, and lunged at Kissler.

The pistol in the gambler's hand exploded with a muffled roar. Nella screamed, staggered back, began to sink, a broad stain of blood spreading across her chest. In that same fragment of time the table overturned under the swaying, struggling men, sending the lantern crashing to the floor with a bright spurt of flame. Again the weapon, now clutched by both men, fired. Kissler stiffened, released his grip on the pistol, and as flames suddenly began to leap up the wall behind him, fell heavily.

Duke, breathing hard, sweat glistening on his strained features, drew back before the crackling fire. Then, metal box in one hand, the gambler's weapon in the other, he retreated toward the door. His legs came up against the bench that Ferd Kissler had placed there. Pivoting, he kicked it clear, and stepped aside, allowed the driving wind to swing the panel open for him.

★ 26 ★

Rossiter reached the stables, pulled open the door, and stepped inside. The poorly lit runway was empty, but the howl of the wind as it rushed into the barn, scattering straw, paper, and bits of trash along the passageway, brought Giffy, the hostler, out of a side room at once.

"Hey——" he began, and then his voice dropped as he recognized Seth Rossiter.

"Came back for my horse," the lawman said, glancing along the stalls in search of the sorrel.

"Over here," Giffy said, and then added, "I got to thinking after you left that them folks you was looking for might've put their animals in that old stable behind the hotel."

"They hadn't signed in at the hotel," Rossiter said.

"Still maybe could've used the barn. Plenty of folks do, specially them that just drops by for a few minutes and wants to get their stock in out of the weather. Sure might pay you to have yourself a look-see before you go riding out on a night like this'n."

The stableman was right; it would cost only the discomfort of facing the wind and blowing sand while he walked the distance to the barn, standing behind the hotel, he assumed.

"Reckon I'll have a look," he said, and started to turn.

"Go out the back," Giffy said, pointing to the rear of the stable. "It'll be a mite shorter."

Rossiter nodded his appreciation, and walking the length of the barn, let himself out into the night once more. The wind was no kinder or less violent on the north side of the sprawling structure and those buildings in line with it than it was on the south side. Pulling the door tight shut, and keeping his jacket buttoned to prevent its being whipped from him by the strong gusts coming at him from behind, Rossiter moved toward the rear of the hotel.

After a dozen yards or so he encountered two men approaching from the residential area and going, no doubt, to while away the evening in one of the saloons. Bodies bowed, lowered faces covered by bandannas, they failed to see the lawman in the choking, swirling darkness, although they crossed his path no more than a stride or two ahead.

He saw the hotel's barn shortly after that and veered to it. The door was unlocked and banging monotonously against its heavy timber facing as he reached it, and stepping inside, he pulled it closed and secured it with a wire hook provided for such.

Halting in the short runway off which a half-a-dozen stalls had been built, Rossiter called out. There was no response, and concluding that no one was in attendance, he struck a match and searched along the compartments for the first horse—if any.

There was one—but it was a black. The adjacent stall contained a bay—but in the next one the lawman located the gray that he had rented back in Cherryville for Duke Finley to use.

A long, gusty sigh slipped from Seth Rossiter's lips, and blowing out the match now scorching his fingertips, he stood quietly in the smelly, noise-filled barn and considered what lay before him.

Duke and the other two—Brodie's widow and a man called Kissler—were there in Saddlerock. They had not been at the hotel, thus they would have to be in one of the saloons along the street. They had not continued as he had thought—that was definite; instead, they were right there in the settlement, either to pick up the money or wait out the storm. Rossiter reckoned he owed Griffy, the hostler, a big thanks for telling him about the hotel's stable. He had been on the verge of riding on.

Pivoting on a heel, the lawman retraced his steps to the door, and opening it, stepped out into the gusty night. There was but one thing he could do—start at the end of the street and make every saloon along the way. And he'd best not pass up the hotel; Duke and his friends just might have checked in after he'd been there.

Crossing the barren area behind the stores, Rossiter reached the rear of the first structure, walked its length, and came to the street. Rounding the corner, he halted at the entrance to the building—a clothing store, he saw from the sign. The windows were blocked and the door locked tight.

Moving on, he tried the next but again found the place closed up and no one around. The succeeding—Dora's—showed signs of life. Pushing open the door, he entered to face a wall of warm smells, thick smoke, and a large woman who came forward behind the bar to greet him.

"You drinking or getting out of the wind?"

"Drinking," Rossiter replied, glancing over the few patrons and seeing no familiar face. "Whiskey."

The woman—he took her to be Dora—reached under the counter, procured a bottle of liquor and glass. She poured the drink, set it before him, and stepped back.

"One hell of a night, ain't it?" she said genially. "Sure ain't no time to be traveling."

"For a fact," the lawman agreed, paying for his whiskey. "Got me wondering about some folks I figured would be around here—two men and a woman—"

"Was here," Dora said, "But they've gone. Left about a half hour ago—that is, if we're talking about the same people. One of them called hisself Duke. Was a noisy sort of a fellow."

"They're the ones," the lawman said, satisfaction coursing through him. Tossing off his drink, he added: "You know where they went?"

"Nope, never asked. Duke paid the bill after they'd done some eating and drinking and then asked me for a lantern. Left right after that. Sure couldn't't've been going far, not with the wind blowing like it is."

An elderly man standing close by at the bar leaned forward. "You talking about them folks that was setting at a back table earlier?"

"Just who we're meaning," Dora replied. "You know where they went, Otey?"

"Well, I seen them going up the street when I was coming out of Ben Adams' store and wondered just where they was heading. Then I seen a light come up in that old shack the other side of the livery stable."

Dora frowned. "Now, why the hell would they go there? That place's been nailed up tight for a long time—but I reckon they had a reason."

"Expect they did," Rossiter said as things began to fall into place in his mind. Nodding to the woman and to Otey, the man who had volunteered information, he went back to the door and stepped out onto the board sidewalk.

Again facing the wind, he started for the opposite end of the row of buildings. The shack, Otey had said, was on the other side of Giffy's Livery Stable. He hadn't noticed it before but it was somewhat difficult to notice anything on such a night.

When he was abreast the hotel, Rossiter paused, looked ahead. A thin yellow streak of light escaping a window's covering broke the darkness beyond the stable. There was someone in the shack, all right— someone who had been inside but a short time. If there had been light at the window earlier, the lawman knew he would have seen it. That someone inside undoubtedly was Duke.

Rossiter stiffened as the muzzle of a gun jammed into his spine. He felt a hand grasp the collar of his jacket, propel him forward.

"Just keep going, Sheriff," a voice close to his ear and coming from behind ordered harshly. "You're going after Duke—and you're taking me with you."

The lawman's jaw hardened. The voice was as familiar as his own name. "Antrum! What the hell's this all about?"

"About a lot of money, that's what," the deputy replied. "Duke and that woman's supposed to pay me five hundred dollars for helping him escape—"

"You helped them?" Rossiter said angrily. "For God's sake, why? You're a lawman!"

"Like I said—for money—for five hundred dollars. They was going to pay me later, after they got that thirty thousand dollars Duke hid, but I got to thinking I ought to have more—was entitled to it for all I done. A quarter of the thirty thousand, at least. Decided then I wouldn't wait on them, because they just might cheat me out of everything. Followed—"

"You're the one that's been trailing Jubal and me—"

"Yeh, reckon I am. Stayed way back so's you'd not figure out who I was, but kept you in sight all the time so's you'd lead me to Duke. . . . Keep going, Sheriff—"

But Rossiter ignored the order, halted, a strong suspicion now running through him. "What about Jubal? You see him?"

"Yeh, I seen him, all right."

Something in Antrum's tone brought a hardness to Rossiter's features. "You kill him?"

"Well, I ain't saying yes and I ain't saying no. Had to shoot him cause he was aiming to stop me."

"If you killed him, I'll see that you swing for it," Rossiter said in a cold, level voice. He was glancing about into the dark, seeking a way to escape the one-time deputy, but with the pistol's muzzle pressing into his back, and the man's firm grip on his collar keeping him off balance, the odds were all against breaking clear.

"Move," Antrum said bluntly, and jabbed hard with his gun barrel again. As the lawman resumed his slow steps, he added, "Where we going? Where's he holed up?"

"I don't know where Duke is," Rossiter answered, thinking fast, "and I'm going after my horse and heading north after him."

"Don't try them lies on me, Sheriff!" Antrum said, once more using his pistol. "You found out where him and them others was when you was in that saloon back there—and you're a-going there now. I didn't run my horse into the ground and steal another'n from a trail drive just so's I could get here and listen to you lie. I got here in a hurry so's I could get my share of that money."

"Who said Duke hid the money around here?" the lawman asked, walking slowly, still desperately trying to come up with a plan for escape. They were abreast the livery stable now and he slid a hopeful glance at the closed doors, wishing that Giffy might open them, create a few moments of distraction that would enable him to act.

"Was Duke told me," Antrum said. Face tipped down so that his hat brim might shield it from the stinging force of the wind, his words were difficult to hear. "I snuck him in a bottle of whiskey one night when you was out of town. He got powerful drunk, and then after he went to sleep, he got to talking and kept saying something about Saddlerock.

"Didn't make no sense to me then, and it never did till I was leaving that last town down the way—Longhorn. Then it come to me, quick like. The next town up the line was called Saddlerock—and he got to raving about it that night because it was where he'd cached all that money. That's when I started riding hard to catch up. Just barely did, too. Only rode in a hour or so ago. . . . That old shack there—it's the last place on the street. That where Duke is? That where we—"

As if in answer, a gunshot, muffled and flat, sounded within the shack. Lamplight flared brightly in the cracks around the window and door, and then came another report.

"That's them, all right!" Antrum shouted. "They're fighting over the money!"

Rossiter stumbled sideways as he was yanked off balance. He reeled when the deputy struck him hard on the side of the head with his pistol. And then, as he started to go down full length onto the wind-scoured street, he became aware that Antrum was lunging toward the shack.

The man's frantic voice reached him through the noisy night. "I want my share of that money! Ain't nobody going to beat me out of it!"

★ 27 ★

The door of the shack flung wide. Duke Finley, a roaring sheet of flame behind him, pistol in one hand, cash box in the other, stood framed in the opening. In that same moment Burt Antrum reached the front of the cabin.

"The money!" Rossiter heard him yell. "I want my share—"

Duke's arm came up. The blast of his pistol sounded above the crackling of the fire mounting fiercely inside the old wood and tarpaper structure. Burt Antrum rocked back from the impact of the heavy bullet at such close range. He spun, then fell, sprawling across the small board landing that fronted the doomed building.

Rossiter, again on his feet, senses cleared, took a step toward the burning shack. Duke had not moved, still stood silhouetted in front of the open doorway into which the wind was pouring and fanning the flames to greater ferocity.

"Duke—get away from there!"

The outlaw started forward, seemingly aroused by the lawman's shout and aware of his danger. Abruptly the trapped, heated air inside the cabin expanded beyond confinement. There was a loud explosion as it disintegrated, hurling bits of flaming wood, tarpaper, and glowing sparks into the black night, where they were caught up by the driving wind and carried onto the adjoining buildings.

Rossiter had a glimpse of Duke Finley being blown forward as the sky began to glow with firelight. He saw the outlaw go face down into the street, and then, still clutching his pistol and the money box, lunge to his feet. There had been no sign of Rube Brodie's widow or the gambler, Ferd Kissler. They, he assumed, had been inside the cabin when it went up, most likely already dead.

"Duke!" he yelled once more, making himself heard above the roaring of the flames. "Throw down that gun and walk toward me!"

The outlaw dropped into a crouch. Head thrust forward, wisps of smoke coming from his clothing where sparks were smoldering, he peered through the swirling haze at the lawman standing on the fringe of the flickering light.

"It's me—Rossiter! I'm taking you on to—"

"The hell you are, Seth!" Finley shouted and triggered a quick shot.

The lawman had anticipated Duke's reaction. Even as Finley's arm came up, he threw himself to one side, drew his weapon, and fired. Duke pitched forward and fell heavily.

Pistol still in his hand, Rossiter hurried to where the outlaw lay motionless. He was fully aware of the spreading fire, of the wind-driven, raging flames that were hungrily devouring other buildings along Saddlerock's street, but he gave it no thought; his mind was centered on the job at hand—on Duke Finley.

Bending down, he rolled the outlaw over onto his back, felt for a pulse as he studied the slack features of the man who had once been his good friend. There was nothing he could do; Finley was dead.

Rising, the lawman turned his attention to the town. The settlement was bathed in a lurid glare. Most of the buildings were burning, and he could see men running in and out of some as they sought to save precious or otherwise important items.

Saddlerock didn't stand a chance, Rossiter saw that as he hurried to help Giffy drive confused and milling horses from the corral behind the stable, where they had gathered after being hazed from the barn, out into the open fields. Then he hurried on to do whatever else he could for the settlement.

The fire had started at the east end of the town, and the wind never once slackening its intensity, and coming also from that direction, had scattered flaming embers over the entire row of buildings that lined the street. Only the church and the homes that were well away from the business area were spared.

With the coming of sunrise, the wind, as if ashamed of its part in the destruction, faded and slipped away, leaving only ashes and charred timbers as reminders of its visit.

Rossiter, soot-streaked, singed, holes in his clothing where live coals had fallen upon him while he labored with others to halt the flames, brushed wearily at his eyes as he stood off to one side and looked at what was left of the town.

It was all because of three outlaws and their greed, and where one of them had intended for two to die, leaving him with all of the money, he had brought about the deaths of four others—Burt Antrum and three townspeople—along with the deaths of his partners and himself. And a town had died, too.

Giffy, standing nearby staring at the still-smoking ruins of his livery stable, shook his head. "I just can't believe it," he said in a dazed voice. "I just can't believe it's happened! There ain't nothing left—nothing! Nobody's got nothing! It was that damned wind blowing so God-awful hard and spreading that fire. How'd it start? You know?"

Rossiter dug into a pocket for his star and pinned it onto his scorched shirt. "Outlaws—in that old shack that was at the end of the street. I don't know exactly what happened, but they must've got to fighting over the money—thirty thousand dollars—that one of them had hidden there.

"A lamp got knocked over, probably, and set the shack on fire. Was some shooting, too, and the woman and one of the men never came out of the place—were most likely dead when it started burning."

Giffy was considering the lawman's star soberly. "And you was chasing after them—"

"Trailed them all the way from Cherryville. I was responsible for one of them—Duke Finley. Was taking him to the pen when he got away from me. Had to get him back and put him behind bars, finish the job."

The stableman nodded, grinned wryly. "I reckon you can say the job's finished now, all right."

Seth Rossiter glanced back up the street to where Finley lay, the box of stolen money still clutched in his nerveless fingers. It wasn't over yet; he would have to return the money to the bank and deliver Duke's body to the warden at the penitentiary—then it would be finished.

"Not quite," he said, "but if you'll help me round up my horse and find the gray that Finley was riding, I'll load up and be on my way."

Ray Hogan is an author who has inspired a loyal following over the years since he published his first Western novel *Ex-marshal* in 1956. Hogan was born in Willow Springs, Missouri, where his father was town marshal. At five the Hogan family moved to Albuquerque where Ray Hogan still lives in the foothills of the Sandia and Manzano mountains. His father was on the Albuquerque police force and, in later years, owned the Overland Hotel. It was while listening to his father and other old-timers tell tales from the past that Ray was inspired to recast these tales in fiction. From the beginning he did exhaustive research into the history and the people of the Old West and the walls of his study are lined with various firearms, spurs, pictures, books, and memorabilia, about all of which he can talk in dramatic detail. Among his most popular works are the series of books about Shawn Starbuck, a searcher in a quest for a lost brother, who has a clear sense of right and wrong and who is willing to stand up and be counted when it is a question of fairness or justice. His other major series is about lawman John Rye whose reputation has earned him the sobriquet The Doomsday Marshal. 'I've attempted to capture the courage and bravery of those men and women that lived out West and the dangers and problems they had to overcome,' Hogan once remarked. If his lawmen protagonists seem sometimes larger than life, it is because they are men of integrity, heroes who through grit of character and common sense are able to overcome the obstacles they encounter despite often overwhelming odds. This same grit of character can also be found in Hogan's heroines and, in *The Vengeance of Fortuna West*, Hogan wrote a gripping and totally believable account of a woman who takes up the badge and tracks the men who killed her lawman husband by ambush. No less intriguing in her way is Nellie Dupray, convicted of rustling in *The Glory Trail*. Above all, what is most impressive about Hogan's Western novels is the consistent quality with which each is crafted, the compelling depth of his characters, and his ability to juxtapose the complexities of human conflict into narratives always as intensely interesting as they are emotionally involving. His latest novel is *Soldier in Buckskin*.